On the Ropes

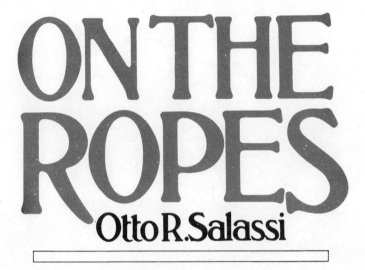

ON THE ROPES

Otto R. Salassi

GREENWILLOW BOOKS

New York

Copyright © 1981 by Otto R. Salassi
All rights reserved. No part of this
book may be reproduced or utilized in
any form or by any means, electronic or
mechanical, including photocopying,
recording or by any information storage
and retrieval system, without permission
in writing from the Publisher,
Greenwillow Books, a division
of William Morrow & Company, Inc.,
105 Madison Ave., New York, N.Y. 10016.

Printed in the United States of America
First Edition   10 9 8 7 6 5 4 3 2 1

Library of Congress
Cataloging in Publication Data
Salassi, Otto R   On the ropes.
Summary: On the death of their mother,
Squint, age 11, and Julie, age 17, are
reunited with their itinerant father
who moves back home with a troupe of
wrestlers, leading them into many
dramatic and comic episodes.
[1. Wrestlers—Fiction] I. Title.
PZ7.S1478On   [Fic]   80-20399
ISBN 0-688-80313-X

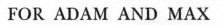

FOR ADAM AND MAX

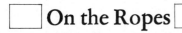 **On the Ropes**

1: Squint's Inheritance

It's always a terrible thing when your mother dies, and I wish this story didn't have to begin where it does, with a funeral and all. But when your mother dies and you're almost alone in the world, well, that's a fact that makes a lot of other facts happen. One thing just stems from another.

It was early summer, 1951, and it was drizzling rain. For that part of East Texas it was a good, slow, farmer's rain, good for the sweet potatoes and for the creeks and cattle. It was a good day for almost everything but a funeral; still, there they were, about two dozen of them, all standing huddled under umbrellas in what had to be the world's worst gumbo mud. Squint Gains, eleven years old and standing in the front row of mourners at the graveside, had three inches of mud sticking to the soles and heels of his boots and was afraid that somebody behind him was going to lose his balance and boost him off his mud stilts into the hole.

He wanted to move, but he couldn't go to the left because on his left stood his aunt Viola, who played the viola and was planning to teach Squint and Julie as soon as she got them home with her to Galveston. He couldn't move in the direction to the right because on his right was his sister Julie, and she couldn't move because next to her was their other aunt, Lucille. Aunt Lucille was the most likable of the two possible adopters, but you couldn't stand to look at her in the face. She had an extra-wide mouth that stretched from one side to the other, and she always kept it moving, like she was licking her teeth with her tongue or something.

It was Squint's first funeral, and his last. If he ever died himself, he'd crawl off to the woods like a cat or an Indian. He'd hide in the potato patch, and nobody would find him till it was too late. If it was the right time of the year and the potatoes were rotting, they'd never find him.

At the head of the grave was a wobbly card table. On the table was a cardboard box of dirt that somebody had covered with its own umbrella. Next to the table and dirt was Brother Lawrence Rambo, who was delivering the sermon, which was all about heaven and what a wonderful place it was. When everybody who was going to heaven got there, all the problems they had on earth were going to seem silly. Poor Constance Gains was up in heaven now, and all her problems were over. That should make everybody who knew her feel good.

Except, of course, it didn't. Squint was old enough to know that problems didn't just disappear, they were passed on to somebody else, and in this case they'd been passed on to him. He and Julie had a father, Claudius Gains, only Claudius had run off and deserted them. That had been right after the war, when Squint was only five and Julie was eleven, six years ago, and nobody could now say rightly where Claudius was. That was the cause of his first problem. Squint didn't want to get adopted by anybody, and neither did Julie. Julie was out of school and pretty enough to get married to anybody in Tyler she wanted. She wouldn't let herself get adopted. As for himself, he was almost twelve and he knew well enough how to take care of himself. He could drive the truck and knew a few things about getting along in the world. Herman had taught him how to cook, and he knew more about sweet potato farming than he wanted to know. He wouldn't let anybody adopt him either. He'd take off for Florida or someplace.

He'd never been to Florida, but that didn't mean he couldn't go. If he didn't get to go to Florida, it would be because of Herman, their farmhand and 450-pound cook. Herman wasn't no kin to Squint and Julie, though he was almost the same as. He'd come on the farm during the war, when he was twenty years old and old enough to fight, but already too fat for the Army to take him. The Army didn't have anything to fit him, and there wasn't too much outside the Army that fitted him either. The suit he wore to the funeral had been specially sewn by the ladies of the church so he might appear decent at the service, and it was about two sizes too small. If Herman couldn't get a job cooking for somebody, he'd starve, and it would be on Squint's conscience.

The funeral was almost over, the graveside part of it. The last thing they had to do was walk by the cardboard box and throw a handful of dirt in the grave, which they all did. Squint watched Herman to see what he did, and Herman did pretty much what Squint thought he'd do. All funeral long he'd been holding the umbrella in his left hand; he'd squeezed his right hand down in his pants pocket, and the hand must have been without circulation for twenty or thirty minutes. Then, when he took it out to throw the dirt, the pocket came out with it, and there he stood, not knowing what to do with the dirty hand, not wanting to mess up the nice suit the church ladies had sewn.

Deacon Rambo finally said, "Now let us take refuge in the church," and Squint thought all the mourners were going to cheer. They would have, too, under different circumstances, if it hadn't been a funeral. They didn't just go back to the church; they tried to march back in the Lord's dignity, but it was difficult with the mud building up on their feet faster than they could kick it off. Squint had Aunt Viola on one arm and Aunt Lucille on the other. Even over the mud and the wet wool, he could smell their perfume and powder. Ahead of him Deacon Rambo was carrying Julie's arm like it was broken and he was protecting it. Somebody in the back of the line stumbled and said, "Texas."

The funeral ordeal continued inside the church with inspirational singing by the church's Good News Choir and Men's Auxiliary Quartet. The quartet, four bony-armed men wearing black short-sleeved shirts with their names embroidered over the pockets—Brother Bob, Brother Jasper, Brother Cecil, and Brother John—stood in front of the choir and hummed in low, rumbling, mournful tones. The Good News Choir was in black choir robes and had arranged themselves in the choir loft like ten bowling pins, their hands crossed over their breasts, their eyes looking toward heaven. They hummed the high parts to go with the quartet's low parts while everybody came in from the graveyard and got seated. The first pew had been reserved for Squint, Julie, and the aunts and uncles.

Two or three songs, and it would be over. There wasn't anything to do but listen to the humming and wait. "Sit still and quit squinting," Julie whispered to him. Both aunts were looking at him and frowning.

He couldn't help squirming because the humming was making him nervous. He couldn't help squinting because that was what he did when he was thinking hard or worrying. That was how he got his nickname, and if worrying over getting adopted or running away to Florida wasn't enough, he had still a third trouble on his mind. He had been through his mother's things, and he'd found her will giving the farm and house to him and Julie. But he'd also found the copy of a loan agreement with the Tyler National Bank, and an eviction notice from the bank giving them till the end of the month to pay the $6,319 that was owed or get evicted. His mother had been keeping them going by selling off the land till there wasn't but eighty acres and the old farmhouse left, and she'd borrowed money on that. There wasn't but seventeen days left in the month to come up with the money.

Brother Cecil started the singing. He stepped forward from the rest of the quartet and looked at Squint and sang four quiet words, "She is not dead . . ." and held the last note of "dead." Then the women in the choir answered him with: "She's only sleeping. . . ." Brother John was next. He stepped forward with Brother Cecil, and they sang it again, looking at Squint and Julie. "She is not dead . . ." and the women answered again: "She's only sleeping. . . ." Four times they did it, till all of the quartet had stepped forward and were looking at Squint and Julie. Then all four of them did it together, and went on to something else.

From where he was sitting, Squint could see out the window to the graveyard, where two men were working with shovels to save as much of the dirt as possible before the rain carried it down the hill. Constance might be only sleeping, but it was Squint's best guess that she was not. If she was only sleeping, then she was going to be sleeping a long, long time, and if anything was going to be done about the problems she left behind her on earth, it was going to have to be done by him.

2: The Telegram

"Read it again, child," Aunt Viola said.

They were sitting in the living room. After the funeral they had come back to the farm to eat dinner and found a telegram in the screen door. The farm is three miles from Tyler on a blacktop road, but where you turn off to come to the house, there isn't any road at all, just dust or mud depending on what the weather's doing. There's usually some kind of rut to show how to get over the field, only the boy who delivered the telegram hadn't been able to follow it. They could tell somebody had visited the house by the misadventures they could see in the mud. He'd been on a motorcycle, it was plain to see, and he'd mired it once and fallen down twice. If the farm had any close neighbors, they'd have heard him cussing no doubt. Squint could look at the signs and see him cussing. The boy had done a good job, though; there wasn't any mud on the telegram except in the right corner, where he'd had to touch it to take it out of his pouch.

Their own shoes and boots were covered, and they had to take them off on the porch. Squint took clues from people to how they were likely to act later on by watching what they did at the time. He watched Aunt Viola and Aunt Lucille watch as Herman took off his boots, and it didn't take a genius to see that there wasn't any future for Herman in either of their lives. They saw Herman's big hairy toes sticking out the ends of his socks, and both of them made faces that would stop rivers.

It was addressed to Julie—the telegram. She waited until they all were inside; then she opened it and read it quietly to herself. Squint watched her expression to get a clue to how he should react when she handed it to him, but he couldn't tell much from it. She gave it to him, and he read it quickly and handed it back to her without comment.

Then she read it aloud to both aunts and uncles, and Squint watched them to see what they thought. Uncle Claude looked relieved, and Uncle George looked like somebody had just walked up to him on the street and handed him a handful of money. It was lucky that Aunt Lucille and Aunt Viola were standing in front of the sofa because both of them suddenly lost all the feeling in their legs and had to sit down. They'd been crying off and on during the funeral, and now both started up again. They went after their noses with their handkerchiefs and took turns honking.

Except for the crying and the blowing of noses, it was quiet. Instead of looking at each other, everybody in the room looked at the pictures on the wall over the mantel. There were four pictures: one of Squint when he was a baby in a Sweetpea nightgown, one of Julie that was taken when she was about ten, one of Constance that was obviously taken to show off her stern, simple-living sense of conviction, and one of Claudius smiling, his World War II medal pinned to the lapel of his frock-tailed coat.

Aunt Viola was the first to stop sobbing and say something. She said, "Read it again, child, and you, Claude, you say what you think we ought to do."

Julie read it again—HAVE LEARNED ABOUT CON-STANCE'S DEATH STOP WILL ARRIVE AFTER FUNERAL TO TAKE CARE OF CHILDREN STOP CLAUDIUS and Uncle Claude scratched his shoulder. He pulled on his ear and squeezed his nose; then he said what he thought they should do. "Don't seem like nothing we can do," he said. "They're Claudius's kids, and he's coming to do his duty by them. I say we've paid our respects, so let's just head on home." Aunt Viola wasn't prone to take his advice too often, but he was hopeful.

Uncle George was just as hopeful. "Don't you think so, too, Lucille? Ain't we done about all we can?"

They had long drives back to Galveston and Waco ahead of them, and this time the women listened to their husbands. Aunt Viola was the maddest, steaming up from the couch and stopping at the front door just long enough to give a final glare to Claudius's picture over the mantel. Aunt Lucille said, "Take me home,

George," and out the door she went.

They didn't even wait for dinner. They all put on their shoes and said their good-byes on the porch, telling the children to let them know if they needed any help whatsoever, no matter what it was, and guaranteeing them that they would be constantly in their prayers. There were final hugs and crying, but soon the aunts and uncles were in their cars and waving as they drove off.

Herman had cooked a big ham for dinner, putting it in the oven that morning before they went to the funeral home. The three of them ate over half of it that evening, on sandwiches with mustard and big slices of dill pickle.

After supper and dishes they were back in the living room, and Squint must have been squinting because Julie told him to quit. He was pacing the room from the lace curtains on one side to the whatnot shelves on the other, thinking.

Herman came in from the kitchen, wiping flour from his hands with a damp towel. He sat on the sofa and tied the towel to the strap of his coveralls and said, "I put a pie in the oven in case Claudius comes in hungry. When do you think he might get here?"

Outside, it was already dark. Squint went to the hall closet and came back in pulling the old cardboard box that he'd found earlier. It was a Pasquale's Home-grown Tomatoes box; one side was split, and one of the flaps on top was ripped. He had to pull it carefully over the carpet to keep it from disintegrating alto-gether.

"All the telegram said was 'after the funeral,' " Julie said. She, like Herman, was watching Squint.

"He ain't coming," Squint said.

It took a few minutes for that to settle in, and while they were confused, he opened the box and started taking the stuff from it. It was filled with Constance's legal papers and keepsakes—the will and eviction no-tice, her and Claudius's marriage license, other legal stuff, some letters, pictures—and held together by a paper clip were six picture postcards.

"And how do you know he's not coming?" Julie asked.

"Because I sent the telegram," Squint said. The pic-ture postcards were what he was looking for. He put everything back in the box and closed the lid; then he started laying the postcards out on the carpet in order by the date of their postmarks.

"You want to tell us why?" she said. She and Her-man got up and came over to where he was working on the floor. He looked at his sister and made a motion with his mouth like he was cleaning his teeth, imitat-ing Aunt Lucille.

"Don't make fun of her; she can't help it."

"You didn't want to go live with them, did you?" Squint was proud of himself for getting rid of them like he did. She shook her head no, and he said, "Then it's settled."

The six postcards were in order. The first one had been sent in 1946, from San Diego, and had a picture of a fighting cock on it. It had been mailed on June 1. The second one was from Las Vegas, mailed on June 1, 1947, and it carried a picture of a slot machine. The third one on June 1, 1948, had been mailed from Juárez, Mexico, and pictured a jai alai contest. All the postcards, in fact, had been mailed on June 1, Constance and Claudius's wedding anniversary, and all of them had a picture of some kind of sporting or gambling scene. The last one had been mailed June 1, 1951, less than two weeks before, and it showed the picture of a racehorse in the winner's circle with a ring of roses around its neck.

The telephone rang two long rings and one short, their ring, and Julie went to answer it.

Herman picked up the postcard with the picture of the horse and looked at it. "I remember when it came," he said, "I went down to the mailbox and got it and gave it to her on the front porch. All she did was look at it. Then she went in the living room and took down her Bible and sat in her chair for hours, not saying anything, just reading the Bible and staring at his picture on the wall."

"Deacon Rambo," Julie said when she came back from the phone, making a face to show that the call had been unpleasant. "He just wanted us to know he was going to pray for us all night." She took the postcard from Herman's hand.

" 'Dear Constance,' " she read, " 'The name of this horse is Praise the Lord and he paid $5.20 to win. It would have done your heart good to hear the crowd cheering him on.' "

"Read the postmark," Squint said.

Julie turned the postcard in her hand and deciphered the blurred word. "D-a-l-l-a . . . Dallas."

"That's where we start looking," Squint said.

3: The Big Potato

Squint was an inventor. He had, when he was nine, taken the wheels off a pair of old roller skates and fastened wooden blocks in their place so that when he strapped them on his feet, he had an extra six inches of reach. He'd watched his mother drive the truck: You turn the key and give the engine some gas, and it starts; you push in on the clutch, and that lets you put it in gear; first gear gets you rolling; second gear lets you go faster; third gear is for moving along. All you needed to drive was a little intelligence and long enough legs. With the seat moved all the way forward and with a pillow under him so he could see over the dashboard, he had learned to drive in the dusty field in front of the house.

When he was ten, he made his first trip to Tyler, to see the movie *Twelve O'Clock High.* To Tyler and back was easy once you got used to driving with other cars on the road, but the sign on the side of the road said DALLAS—16 MILES, and he was starting to get worried. He'd made it through Noonday, Chandler, Brownsboro, Murchison, Athens, Eustace, Mabank, Kemp, Kaufman, and Crandall, but those places weren't nothing but speck eyes on a potato, and Dallas was the big potato itself. It was a potato you could take to the fair.

"Reach in your sack, and hand me the glasses and nose," Squint told Julie. Julie'd wanted them all to leave the truck in Tyler and ride the bus, but that would've cost too much money since she and Herman, like two silly geese, had insisted on going with him. Herman rode in the back and brought more attention than they needed, or wanted, by making the truck lean to whichever side he sat on. The false glasses and nose were to make Squint look older in case they got looked at by the police. He didn't want to get arrested before he got there.

"Praise the Lord," he said, laughing. "Don't you

just know that got her goat?"

"We may not be able to find him," she said. "He may not even be in Dallas."

"We'll find him." He couldn't tell her how he knew, but it was a sixth sense he had about Claudius. He felt like he could walk right up to him, no matter where he was hiding.

"What if we find him and he won't come back home with us?" she said. A girl will find something to worry about, even if she has to invent it.

"He won't have any choice," Squint said. As always, he had a plan.

They came into Dallas and worked their way farther and farther in till they were downtown. There he had to circle the blocks a few times, finding first the building he was looking for, then a place to park in the lot beside it. Julie's eyes got as big as hen eggs when she saw where they were. "Are you crazy?" she said, ducking down in the seat. "This is the police station!"

Squint took off the false face and put it under the seat, then took the skate blocks off and put them under, too. He grabbed the paper sack and got out. Julie and Herman followed him around the building to the front, and on the way he explained it. "When you're looking for somebody and you need help, you go to the police."

One side of the room smelled like someone had mopped it with ammonia; the other side smelled like someone was cooking week-old fish. On both sides of the room, sitting in straight-back chairs, were thugs with bruises on their faces, and JDs with packs of cigarettes rolled in their sleeves. Squint, Julie, and Herman walked through the middle of them to the uniformed sergeant behind the desk. Squint opened the paper sack and took out the framed picture of Claudius in his frock-tailed coat, the one of him smiling and wearing the medal, and showed it to the sergeant. "We're here to report a missing person," he said.

The sergeant didn't say anything, only looked at Squint, Julie, Herman, and the picture.

"We think he might have something to do with sports," Squint went on, and showed him the postcards. He knew from listening to police shows on the radio that it was important to give them all the clues.

4: Monkeyblood

Claudius Gains did indeed have "something to do with sports," but that was like saying flies have something to do with honey or gorillas have something to do with the jungle. What Claudius had learned early in life was that there were some people who liked to perform sports, and there were a lot of other people who were willing to pay money to see the performance. He'd never been a particularly big man, and he hadn't been blessed with great speed or great strength, and he'd never been able to live the clean life or train, so he'd never become a performer. And watching sports was nice enough, but there wasn't any future in it. The future was in the money people were willing to pay, and people would pay to see anything.

"We got 'em," Claudius said, looking at the screaming, jumping, downright dangerous collection of people in the arena. In the stands above the aisle where Claudius was standing, a woman was slamming her black purse into the back of the head of the man in front of her.

"Better get some men over here," he told the man standing next to him. "It's gonna get wild in exactly" —he looked at his watch—"two and a half minutes."

The man who was getting hit had to grab the woman's purse to make her quit. The man behind the woman had to grab her to keep her from falling between the slats.

Now whether you want to call professional wrestling a sport or not is up to you, but there were almost two thousand people in the arena that night who did. They had paid $2 per adult and 50 cents per child to see it, and they liked it rough, tough, and bloody. That's what the crowd wanted, and that's what they were about to get.

There were four wrestlers in the ring: the Masked Marvel, who was partners with the Steel Claw against the Baron, who was partners with Panzer Kaufman. The Baron was as bald as a pumpkin and wore a monocle when he wasn't wrestling. Panzer Kaufman had a scar that ran from his cheek to the middle of his forehead and had his thick gray hair cut in a perfect flattop. The Masked Marvel wore a black mask that covered his whole head and had bright purple circles around the holes for his eyes, nose, and mouth. The Steel Claw was missing his right hand and wrist; where they should have been there was a big hook which looked something like a question mark. The hook was sharp on the end, but it had a hard rubber scabbard covering it so it wouldn't be too dangerous.

In the action that was going on in the ring, the Masked Marvel had the Baron caught in a headlock and, when the referee wasn't looking, was gouging his knuckles in the Baron's good eye. On the other side of the ring, to keep the referee running back and forth between them, the Steel Claw had his hook around Panzer's throat and was choking him. It was the third and final fall in a best two-out-of-three tag-team match, and the Masked Marvel and the Claw were clearly winning. Panzer and the Baron were the crowd favorites, but only because they were older—youth against age, strength against experience. The Masked Marvel and the Claw also cheated a lot, and their cheating didn't sit well with the crowd. But what the crowd knew was that you could cheat only so much without making your opponents mad, and the Baron and Panzer were starting to get mad.

With sheer brute strength, Panzer got his hands around the hook that was choking him and with the strength of a team of mules pulling an oak stump from the middle of a cotton field, Panzer pulled that hook away from his throat, straightened the arm across his shoulder, and walked it steadily toward the ropes. With the strength of ten men he forced the arm over the top rope, held it in place, and brought up the bottom rope to catch the hook. Then he stood on the bottom rope to inflict great pain on the arm. Inspired, he then jumped on the bottom rope with both feet and boosted the Claw out of the ring into the lap of a muscular woman at ringside.

"Beautiful," Claudius said.

Across the arena, a boy, a girl, and two men had come in and were standing near the entrance. Claudius saw them, but it didn't register. Nothing was important right then except what was going on in the ring.

The lap the Claw landed in belonged to a woman

named Betty, who was in real life married to Panzer and part of the act. She broke the Claw's fall, and when he was on his hands and knees in the aisle in front of her, she passed him a small capsule of monkey-blood—red dye and molasses, really, but when the Claw broke the capsule against his eyebrow and came up with red stuff splattered all over his eye and face, there wasn't a person in the stands who wasn't screaming.

He pretended he was blind and stumbled along the aisle, half threatening to fall on the people seated there, then catching his balance and faltering back toward the ring. Above him, Panzer stalked, following him around the corner of the ring, trying to do him even more damage if it were at all possible. The Claw first stepped in a bucket and had that son of a gun stuck on his feet; then he made a mistake of stumbling too close to the ring, and Panzer was able to grab the hook again and stretch it up and hook it on the top rope. That put the Claw in the position of having his right arm stretched out of the socket on one end, being blinded by his own blood in the middle, and having a ring bucket stuck on his foot at the other end. The crowd was in such an uproar if the fight didn't end pretty soon, somebody was going to get killed.

With about ninety seconds left to go in the time period, it got even worse. Out of the stands came Rose, the Baron's wife and a wrestler in Claudius's troupe.

She wasn't going to take any more of the Masked Marvel's gouging her husband in the only good eye nature had left him. Hiking up the leg of her pedal pushers, she delivered a kick to the side of the Mask's head, and he lost his hold. The Baron was free in a quick twist and started pounding the Mask with his forearm while Rose held the Mask's arms behind him.

The referee was, in the meantime, getting after Panzer, threatening him with immediate disqualification if he didn't free the Claw from what was clearly an illegal hold and stop kicking him in the ribs. With about ten seconds left to go, Betty, who was fifty pounds stouter than the referee and two hundred pounds stronger, crawled under the bottom rope and started chasing the rascal around the ring. If he was going to disqualify her husband, he was going to pay for it.

With Panzer trying to keep Betty from eating the referee alive and the Claw free and swinging the sharp hook blindly around the ring, trying to spear Panzer but a threat to everybody, mercifully the bell clanged and the match was over. The referee quickly and wisely raised the arms of Panzer and the Baron in victory. It was all over except the sometimes-tough final act of getting from the ring to the dressing room.

Which was why Claudius had asked the arena manager for more men. It was in the contract that the arena was responsible for furnishing protection from the ring to safety. Claudius guaranteed his wrestlers would provide the excitement; the arena had to provide the protection.

Rose and Betty slipped out while the winners were taking their bows, and Panzer and the Baron got out quickly to the cheers of the crowd, while the Masked Marvel was trying to get close to the monkey-blood-blinded Claw to make him quit trying to kill people with his hook and help him back to the dressing room. If there hadn't been a corridor of squat Legionnaires to hold the people back, they never would have made it. The woman with the purse in the stands above Claudius tried to hit the Claw with it, and the Claw had to swing at her with his hook to get her to back off. The man behind her hit him with a lighted cigar.

The crowd had gotten exactly what it had wanted, Claudius greeted the Claw and Mask with the word "perfection," and that's what it had been. Absolute perfection.

It took awhile for the policeman to get directions on where to go and to get through the crowd to the dressing room on the other side. By the time they got there, the policeman stopping to buy the kids hot dogs and Cokes, feeling sorry for them and being a soft heart, the Claw, the Mask, Panzer, and the Baron had already taken showers and dressed. All professional wrestlers are smart enough to get out of an arena they have played; the quicker they get away from a crowd they have just incited, the better the wrestlers' health.

The Baron was wearing his monocle and his toupee; the Masked Marvel was still wearing his mask because he never took it off, for anybody or anything; Claudius was counting out money to the six of them, their share of the gate, and explaining things.

"We're in," he was explaining.

Outside the dressing room, the next match was in the first fall, but the crowd was still wild. "That's the sound of money out there," Claudius told them. "I talked to the manager, and he wants us back next week with a new act."

They were his children. They depended on him to get them wrestling engagements. He got them jobs and thought up the acts. They were big and bulky and not particularly blessed with anything but each other and their own particular talents, and Claudius took care of them.

The Claw raked in his money with his hook and scratched the finish of the table they were sitting around.

"That's right, scratch everything up," Claudius said. "Can't you be careful with that thing?"

Betty and Rose took their and their husbands' shares, folded the money, and tucked it in their purses. The Mask took his, and Claudius was putting away the rest. Claudius's share was the greatest, almost half, but he was responsible for things like expenses, and without him they wouldn't be making anything.

He was putting away his money in his coat pocket when the door of the dressing room opened and the policeman stuck his head in to see what was going on. Seeing that they were decent, he pushed the door open wider, Claudius saw the girl and the boy up close, and they recognized each other.

To Squint, his father looked like the picture, only older. For years he'd been looking at that picture, wondering what it would say if it could talk. Because the picture was smiling, he always expected it to break out in a laugh at any minute. Now it wasn't a picture, but the real thing, and the first thing it did was sit down in the chair behind it and groan.

"You don't have to tell me," Claudius said, slapping the side of his head with his hand. "Right in the most lucrative period of my life, something terrible is about to happen."

So it was that Squint and Julie were reunited with their father.

5: The Devil's Workshop

There were questions Squint wanted to ask, but expert that he was, he waited for the right time.

They spent the night in a Dallas hotel and then, in the morning, headed back to the farm. Claudius was a bit angry about the policeman, saying, "You didn't have to get the police after me. I'd have come back to help if I'd known you needed it." The policeman had a warrant ordering Claudius's arrest; however, Claudius bought ten tickets to the Dallas Policemen's Ball and thereby avoided spending the night in jail.

Driving the truck back to Tyler and home, Claudius said hardly anything. The rain they'd had two days before was gone, and in its place were the East Texas sun and dust, plenty of dust. Claudius drove without taking his eyes off the road.

Between Noonday and Chandler he'd been stuck behind a stinking Trailways bus. The old truck didn't have the power to pass, not with Herman in the back, and the bus wouldn't speed up or go any slower. Only once did Claudius look up from the road; he looked around at the rolling fields, full of sweet potatoes mostly, but here and there some cotton, and here and there a few derricks. His eyes passed over the landscape, then came to rest on Squint and Julie beside him in the truck. He had decided where to place the fault of his misfortune. "It's Texas," he said. "It ain't your fault, or my fault, or anybody's fault; it's Texas."

Squint told him about the bank and the eviction notice. Claudius nodded but said nothing and went back to staring at the road.

Squint dozed off, and when he woke up, they were stopped at the mailbox to the farm and Claudius was waiting to see that the others hadn't missed the turn. When he saw them coming, he started over the empty field to the house. Following the truck was a green Fleetline Chevy, a '41 but still in good shape, with Panzer driving and the Baron, Betty, and Rose riding with him. Behind that was an old, squatty school bus, painted an olive drab with surplus army paint. The Masked Marvel drove, with the Claw operating the manual windshield wiper so he could see. The Chevy and the bus disappeared in the swirling dust behind the truck, and Squint saw his father smile.

They stopped in front of the house, and in a few seconds the others stopped behind them. The caravan had reached its destination, and everybody got out. The Mask handed the Claw a whisk broom, and the Claw whisked the dust off the back of the mask and around the ears. "Next time we go in front," he said, looking at the way they'd come and then at the house. "Is this it?" he asked.

It, for better or worse, was it.

In the old days, farmers built big houses because
they had big families, full of male children to work
the land. Squint's great-grandfather on his mother's
side, a pioneer, had built a two-story house with seven
bedrooms, and he'd managed to fill it with kids, but
mostly with girls.

Squint's grandfather had done his best but had
given up after three girls in a row, Aunt Lucille, Aunt
Viola, and Constance. Constance inherited the duty of
filling the house and went out and found Claudius,
captured him, as Claudius would later tell them, "like
Clyde Beatty captures his tigers." The white paint was
peeling, and a few of the boards in the porch could
stand replacing, but it was still a good house. The
downstairs rooms were high-ceilinged and wide; upstairs there were rooms like dollhouse rooms, kept fur-
nished and clean for somebody to move into them.

"I'd be tempted to let the bank have it," Claudius
said irritably, "except that I hate banks."

He walked over to the back of the truck and let
down the tailgate and motioned for the Claw to come
to him. The Claw went over, and Claudius had him
hold the hook out; then he loaded it with three suitcases. The other wrestlers unloaded their belongings,
and Claudius led them up the front steps.

Inside, Julie took the wrestlers upstairs and showed

them their rooms; Herman went to the kitchen and
started cooking the evening meal. Claudius was home
for the first time in years, and he stood for a long time
in front of the mantel, looking at the picture of Constance in silence.

"Can I ask you a question?" Squint asked, coming
over to stand near his father.

"If it's not too personal."

It was the question Squint had been waiting the
whole trip to ask, and this, he judged, was the right
moment. "How come you ran away?"

Claudius knew sooner or later he'd have to answer
it. "That's not too personal," he said, "but answer me
one first. What reason did she give?" He nodded at
Constance's picture.

"She just said that the devil calls some people the
same way God calls them, and the devil up and one day
called you."

Claudius smiled. "I'm not going to argue with that.
She was always the one to know what God and the
devil were up to." He continued to look at the picture.
"We were exact opposites," he said. Then he made a
snarling face and flexed his fingers at the picture like
claws. "We got on each other's nerves."

"She took me down in the cellar when I was about
seven to show me the 'tools of the devil,' " Squint said,
"and it was all your things. She kept a padlock on the

door to keep them locked up."

Claudius couldn't believe it. "You mean it's all still there?"

Squint pulled a string from his pocket as Claudius watched. On the end of the string was the key he'd found in Constance's things.

They opened the door to the cellar, and it was like looking into the inner sanctum of a spookhouse. Cobwebs hung so thick that Claudius had to lead the way with a broom. He found the light switch and turned it on, and Squint saw a room full of furniture and boxes covered with sheets. The first thing Claudius uncovered was the pool table in the middle of the room, its green felt faded but otherwise in good condition. It was easy for Squint to see that his father was pleased.

"First chance I get, I'll teach you to play," Claudius said. He pulled a sheet from a stack of boxes and brought the top one to the table. He found a framed picture and showed it to Squint—a picture of ten or twelve tough-looking women and one pretty one and Claudius, all standing around the front of a square-nosed bus. Claudius, looking to be in his twenties, was sitting on the nose of the hood, and over his head and behind him was a big wooden star. It was fixed to the top of the bus and said BUNNY MAPHIS AND HER ALL-

GIRL ALL-STARS. Over the windshield it said TYLER TEXAS.

"Nine hundred and seventy-one wins and only one defeat," Claudius said, smiling at the memory. "They weren't much to look at, but they could play some softball, and there never was a bunch of women more generous."

There was a trophy in the box of a man holding a pool cue. Claudius looked at it for a second, then put it back in the box and covered the top. "You know what the first rule of pool shooting is?" he asked. Squint shook his head no. "Never let anybody know how good you are."

"But you had to let them know to win the trophy, didn't you?" Squint reasoned.

Claudius, who was busy discovering more things, just said, "Left-handed." He'd shot so sloppy to win, the guy he'd beaten demanded they shoot again for money.

There was a pinup calendar from some auto-parts store. Claudius looked at it, then at Squint, and rolled it back up. The next thing he uncovered was a jukebox.

They moved stuff out of the way and rolled it to where Claudius remembered there was a plug. When they plugged it in, Squint thought he'd never seen anything so beautiful. It stood taller than Squint and

gleamed with chrome, and it lit the room and everything in it with all the colors of the rainbow. All Squint
could do was start laughing. It was better than heaven,
better even than Christmas. A thousand times or more
he'd wondered and dreamed about the cellar and the
things that were locked up down there. The pool table,
his mother had told him, was the altar where his father
sacrificed lambs. The pockets were there to collect the
blood.

"Now let's see if she cranks," Claudius said, punch-
ing one of the buttons on top.

A mechanical arm moved from one end of a rack of
records to the other, stopped, then started back. The
arm was jerky and needed some oil, but it stopped
again and pulled one of the records out of the rack and
put it down on the turntable. Something inside the
machine groaned, but it started the record turning,
and the needle arm swung over and touched down.
The record played too fast, then too slow, and it was
too loud. It was guitars and fiddles and drums and
somebody singing; upstairs it must have sounded like
somebody being tortured because everybody came on
the run to investigate.

Herman got there first, followed by Julie, the Mask,
the Claw, and Panzer. They had their hands over their
ears, and nobody could hear anything, so Claudius unplugged it. "Just needs some adjustment," he said.

It turned into a party then, with everybody pulling sheets off things and showing them to each other. Julie discovered a barber chair with a lot of contraptions welded to it, and Claudius got in to show them how it worked. It went up and down like a regular barber chair, it could lie backwards and the footstool would come up so you could stretch out, and it could spin around. A platform welded to the seat on the right side held a metal ice chest. There was a reading lamp fixed on the back, and mounted on the left arm, so you could swing it back and forth, was a wooden platform that served as a desk, and mounted on the desk were a portable radio and another device that Squint didn't recognize. The cords from the radio and the other device ran under the desk and under the arm to a junction with the lamp cord in back. Right behind the arm was a heavy iron pipe which served as a holder for a canopy.

Not a canopy exactly—more like a big umbrella that people use at beaches. Herman found it folded in a corner, and he and the Mask got it in place. The Claw reached up under it to raise it up and got his hook caught in one of the spokes.

"I'm going to take a hacksaw to that thing one of these days," Claudius told the Claw. The Claw got the hook free, and then Claudius showed them how he could plug in a socket that went to a line that ran up the pole from the inside and hung over the top. They plugged that in at the wall, and Claudius tested the lamp. It worked, the radio worked, and the other thing worked as well. The other thing was a Miller High Life Beer advertisement that had little bouncing balls of colored light. If you watched the lights too long at a time, you'd get hypnotized.

Julie and some of the others thought the chair was silly, but to Claudius it was the only thing in his life that he'd ever gotten just the way he wanted it, and he was serious about it. He could sit upright and look at the bouncing lights, listen to the radio, and drink cold beer without getting up. Or he could lie back and listen to the radio and study the picture that was glued to the underside of the umbrella, a picture of Napoleon with his hand sticking inside his coat.

"I couldn't decide for a long time what kind of picture I wanted up there. Then I thought: This chair is for serious thinking, and I never could look at Napoleon without thinking about something." Claudius looked at the picture, and Squint could see his mood change. "Unplug it," he said, and the Baron unplugged the chair.

Claudius got out then and lowered the umbrella and took it out of the holder. With the umbrella over his shoulder and everybody else watching him, he started up the stairs. "Grab up the chair, and follow me," he said, and the Baron and Panzer, Herman and the Mask carried it up the stairs.

They ran an extension from the side porch to a birdhouse on a pole about thirty-five yards away. There, near the bottom of the pole, they set up the chair and plugged it in for Claudius, who got in. "The sooner I get started, the better," he announced. "I don't want anybody to bother me for a while."

So the homecoming party ended, and they went inside to wait.

6: Illustrious Ancestors

It never fails that the bigger the house is, or the more the rooms, the more people are going to congregate in just one of the rooms. In the case of Claudius's tribe, it was the kitchen. The parlor still belonged to Constance; it looked and was treated like one of those historic rooms they set up in museums with velvet ropes to keep people back. The kitchen, on the other hand, belonged to everybody.

They were gathered around the table for the evening meal, the first of meals they would share together. Herman was in heaven. The only thing he liked more than cooking for people was cooking for people who liked to eat as much as he did. Professional wrestlers like to eat. Panzer, the Baron, Betty, and Rose had a stack of bare corncobs in front of them that was easily a foot high. The Mask and the Claw, still young and growing boys, had eaten fourteen of the corncobs in the pile. An entire mountain of mashed potatoes disappeared from the turkey roasting pan it had been served in. Among the six of them, they'd manage to consume two whole meat loaves and a child's-size mud bath of gravy. If they hadn't been professional wrestlers, they might have been professional eaters. When the main meal was over, they were ready for dessert.

Squint didn't care for any. He left the table and stood looking out the screen door; Julie watched him because he was squinting again and she didn't like to see her brother worry. Outside, it was dark, and there wasn't much moon, but Squint could still see the shape of the chair. He could see the bouncing pinpoints of light from the Miller sign and hear, he thought, the radio playing.

"Is he still out there thinking?" Julie asked from the table.

"About ninety miles an hour, it looks like," Squint told them. He came back to the table and sat down again.

"I've seen him go like this for days," Panzer said. He, the Baron, and Betty and Rose had been with Claudius the longest, going on three years. The Mask and the Claw were relative newcomers to the troupe. They'd been with it for only about a year. "Usually it's when he needs to think up a new act or we need money. He always comes out of it, though, and he's always got some kind of scheme." Herman had baked an apple cobbler for dessert and launched into it.

The Masked Marvel was sponging up the last of the gravy on his plate. He'd been raised in a strict family where the rule was: "Thou shalt leave no food un-et." As he worked quickly to get to the cobbler before it was gone, he dripped a little gravy down his lip, and it got inside the mask to his chin. With the others at the table watching, he carefully unzipped the zipper in back and pulled it up enough to get to his chin and wipe.

Betty, who was sitting next to him, leaned over as quick as a cat and tried to get a look under it, but the Mask was quicker than she was, and she didn't see anything more than the bottom of his throat. "You're going to have to wash that thing sooner or later; why don't you let me throw it in the machine right now?"

The Mask slipped his mask back in place indignantly, like his honor as a wrestler was being challenged. "I put on this mask when I became the Masked Marvel. Nobody sees my face again, ever." He patted the top of his head and stirred up a small cloud of dust.

"I know what we could do," Rose told Betty. "We could look him up in his high school yearbook the next time we're in Waco."

"I'll save you the trouble," the Mask said, digging out his wallet for his snapshots. He got out three pictures, looked at the first one, and started it around the table. The first one was of his high school band. They were in uniform and holding their instruments; in the back row, holding a bass drum and wearing his mask, was the Mask. The second picture was a graduation picture, with him wearing the mask. The third picture had been doctored with black construction paper and glue and showed a little baby, not more than three or four weeks old, wearing a mask. Everybody at the table was laughing except Julie, who only smiled. Squint saw a look in her eyes that he'd never seen before, and he was more than familiar with the variety of her looks.

They hung around the kitchen till bedtime. The Claw and the Masked Marvel sat together at one end of the table playing cribbage. The Claw shuffled awkwardly and forever with his left hand while he kept his own score on the board with the sharp point of the hook. He knew the Mask got impatient and made mistakes.

"Why don't you let me deal for you?"

"You'd cheat."

"But why would I cheat? We're not playing for anything but pennies."

"You'd still cheat," the Claw said. It was one of those moments when having a hook came in handy.

The Baron and Panzer were doing the dishes. The Baron was washing, and Panzer was drying.

Julie, wearing her nightgown and a robe, came to the kitchen to brush her hair, but Betty wouldn't hear of it and made Julie sit in a chair while she stood behind her and brushed. Rose watched and was jealous.

The Baron handed Panzer a soapy-slick plate, and it slipped through Panzer's hand; the Baron flicked out his arm and caught the plate before it was halfway to the floor, yawning while he did it. Both Julie and Betty saw it happen, but only Julie was impressed.

"They've only been practicing that act for about thirty years," Betty told her.

The Baron looked at Julie and winked, then handed Panzer another slippery plate, and they repeated the trick.

"Have you all been together that long . . . thirty years?"

"Let me think," Betty said, stopping the brushing while she tried to remember. "The Baron and Rose got married in 1921; we got married in 1919, right after the war, right before Christmas as I remember. We were in love, and broke, and getting married was cheaper than giving presents."

"Did you have children?" Julie wanted to know.

Rose couldn't stand it anymore and came over. "Let me brush a little," she begged, and Betty reluctantly surrendered the brush.

"We've both raised some little wrestlers of our own," Rose took up. "I raised two of them, and Betty raised one. They're all wrestling together on the Missouri circuit."

"It all sounds crazy," Julie said.

"There ain't nothing crazy about it," Betty said. "All eight of our parents were wrestlers, and all of their parents before them."

Squint came into the kitchen from taking his bath, a blanket and pillow under his arm to take out to Claudius.

"I'll take it out to him," Herman said. He had a plate of food warming in the oven and took that out as well.

"The old Greeks used to wrestle each other," Rose said. "Do you suppose our families go back that far?"

"Maybe even farther," Betty said. "I was at the hairdresser's last week, and I read in one of those *National Geographics* where they've found a prehistoric cave in France somewhere, and on the walls they found pictures of cavemen wrestling, and one of the cavemen looked just like my great-uncle."

"I had a cousin on my mother's side who was a Greek," Rose said, laughing. "Used to wrestle in Athens even."

"Athens, Georgia?" Betty asked. They were having more fun than they'd had in years.

"No," Rose told her, "Tennessee."

Claudius was blank, sitting upright in the chair, mesmerized by the bouncing lights. Herman put the food on the desk in front of him, covered him with the blanket, and stuffed the pillow behind his head.

"I'll wait up for him," Herman told Squint. "You go on to bed."

So ended their first night together, with Herman reading the paper and dozing in the kitchen, Claudius outside in his chair, and Squint taking one last look at him from his upstairs window before climbing into bed.

7: The Great Napoleon

A strong commotion in the upstairs hall sent Squint bounding from the bed to the window. The chair was still there; it sent a long shadow across the dusty crabgrass in the early-morning sun, but it was empty of his father. Claudius was in the hall, knocking on door after door to rouse the sleepy inhabitants: the Claw, Panzer, the Baron, Julie, and Squint at the end of the hall. The Masked Marvel stuck his head out of the bathroom, his mask rolled up to his nose to expose the lower part of his face, covered with shaving cream.

Claudius was standing at the top of the stairs. "Meeting downstairs in fifteen minutes," he announced, and Squint had to look at him to believe it.

He was dressed in a black suit that was so fine it might have been skinned off a Baptist preacher. His hair was slicked down on his head like he'd just stepped out of a barber chair. His bright blue silk tie was a human hand wide in the widest part, with a hula dancer in a grass skirt running from just below the knot at the top, her hips swinging out in the widest part, to the bottom. In his hand he carried a derby hat, and Squint had never seen anything more magnificent-looking, at least not that early in the morning. He made a vow to himself that when he grew up, he'd have a tie like that.

When Squint came down, Claudius was scrambling eggs, the tie tucked inside his shirt to keep it from getting splattered or spilled on. At the same time he warmed up a slice of leftover ham in the skillet. Squint judged that his father must have been up awhile to have had time to do all the things he'd done. Besides his being dressed like he was, there was a packed suit-case beside the table, and by the back door there was a cobweb-covered half-empty case of Jax beer.

Herman, Julie, and the others came in then and, like Squint, watched as Claudius set his breakfast on the table, took a can of beer from the refrigerator, and sat down. The wrestlers were not accustomed to seeing Claudius display so much energy so early in the morning. Claudius took a big bite of scrambled eggs and chased it with a swallow of beer.

"First thing," he said, "all that money I gave you in Dallas, I need it back." His derby hat was beside him at the table; he turned it upside down and handed it to Panzer. The Claw and the Mask still had their money on them; the rest was in Betty's and Rose's pocketbooks.

"Second thing," Claudius went on, "as you all know, last night I sat out there and put my mind to work on the problem of money." Everyone waited while he finished the ham and pushed his plate away. "And the human mind, when it's in good working order and energized, is fearful and frightening." He took the last swallow of beer and put the empty can on the plate. Standing, looking at them and radiating purpose, he pointed to his brain and said, "Absolutely frightening."

He picked up the suitcase, and they clamored

through the kitchen after him. As the Claw passed on one side of the table, his hook got caught in the table-cloth. Panzer, walking on the other side, picked up the plate and beer can with such timing that Julie wondered whether that too had been rehearsed.

Claudius stopped them on the front porch and stepped down the three steps to the front yard.

By then it was clear to them all that Claudius was leaving. He was going somewhere, to do something, but where or what he wasn't going to tell them.

"It was the great Napoleon who once said, 'Give me a place but on which to stand, and I will move the earth.'"

Actually it was the great Archimedes. Squint knew that much from reading his *Weekly Reader*.

"What I got to say is just as important." He reached down and picked up a handful of dust and let it powder through his fingers like sand. "I say, 'Out of this desert there shall flow a great fountain, and the waters of that fountain are going to cool our feet and quench our thirsts.'"

Squint hoped he didn't mean that in the order he said it.

Claudius put the suitcase in the back seat of the Chevy and held out his hand for Panzer to give him the key. "From now on, I'm on a tight schedule, and you are, too," he told them. "It would help, while I'm gone, if you move that stuff up from the cellar. Put the pool table in the living room, and you, Claw, you keep that hook away from it." He got in the car and started the engine. "I'll be back in a couple of days if everything goes right. In the meantime, try to stay out of trouble."

Then he drove away, and Squint and the others watched him disappear into a cloud of dust.

"Maybe I ought to have gone with him," Herman said. The wrestlers had already started moving back inside to the kitchen; Julie, Squint, and Herman had remained on the porch, each one thinking the same thing. Claudius had run off before; what was to keep him from doing it again?

"Things are different now," Squint said, although he wasn't sure he could put his finger on the difference.

Later they all were in the living room looking around, all except Herman, who had been captured by the rainbow jukebox in the cellar and was down there staring at it. Betty straightened a doily on the back of a chair, a doily that the Mask had brushed against and scooted out of place. Nothing in the room was out of place. The picture of Claudius had been replaced, but it was Constance's hard chin and unflinching eyes that dominated the room.

"I'm not sure at all we ought to do this," Betty said.

Like Rose, she wasn't overjoyed at the thought of re-arranging a dead woman's room. They looked at Julie, whose decision it rightly was, and Julie looked at Squint.

Squint looked at the picture. "When she was alive, we minded her," he said, and it was true. There might have been some disputes in minor details, such as taking baths and going to school on certain occasions and saying prayers as much as she demanded, but in the main it was true. They had minded their mother.

"I think we ought to mind Claudius now," he said, and Julie considered that advice while everyone waited.

Herman, downstairs, wasn't thinking about nothing. The lights came around red and purple and blue and yellow and orange and red. He wasn't a good man or a bad man, and he wasn't smart enough to judge anybody as to whether they were sinners or not, but it did seem a sin to him that anything as pretty as that jukebox was kept in a dark, dingy cellar. He made up his mind and unplugged it, wrapped the cord so it wouldn't get in his way and get stepped on. Then he grabbed the machine in a bear hug.

"I'm just afraid she's gonna come back and haunt us," Betty said, "and I don't want her haunting me."

On the bottom shelf of one of the biggest whatnots was a figurine family seated around a figurine table eating figurine fruit, and it was like no figurine dust would dare settle on it. Apples, oranges, even little grapes. The Baron couldn't look at it without feeling sad. "This place would drive me crazy," he told them, but they weren't listening.

Herman was coming down the hall carrying the jukebox. He put it down in the living room and stepped back, proud of himself.

If anybody was going to be haunted, it was going to be Herman. Julie said, "Let's do it," and they began.

They made their plans at breakfast, and by noon they'd cleared the living room of the carpet, all the furniture, and everything hanging on the walls. The first thing to go was the picture of Constance from the mantel. Nobody wanted to work in the room with her glaring at them.

Their plan was to take the stuff from the living room and replace it with stuff from the cellar, but they also had to do something with the walls. Everywhere there was a picture, or a whatnot shelf, or a framed embroidery with a wise saying like "What Is a Home Without a Mother?" there was a light spot.

"We're just gonna have to paint it," Betty said.

8: How They Painted the Walls

They sent the Baron and Panzer to town to buy supplies and equipment. They would need brushes and rollers, turpentine, and paint. The paint ought to be white, or off-white, or maybe a nice yellow or light orange for the walls and a dark mahogany for the strip around the windows.

Betty and Rose covered the floor with old newspapers. Herman brought a couple of stepladders in from the barn. The Masked Marvel took down the light fixture in the middle of the ceiling, and he and the Claw hung an overhead fan in its place. The dusty old fan came up from the cellar. It had three-foot wooden blades that spun slowly and clacked quietly like an express train at night.

The Baron and Panzer came back from town with the supplies. The paint had the color of milk of magnesia and the texture of clabbered cream. The Claw opened the cans and stirred the paint with his hook. The Baron, Panzer, and the Mask stripped to their waists and started. The Baron also took off his toupee.

The Mask painted the ceiling, dripping paint all over his mask and all over the floor. He also dripped a little on the Baron's bald head.

The newspaper started sticking to everybody's feet. Betty and Rose were painting the trim. The Mask's mask was getting ruined, so he and the Baron changed places and the Baron started dripping paint on the Mask's head.

The paint fumes started making everybody giddy. Betty painted a mustache on Rose, Rose painted one on Betty, and both of them painted a Kilroy on the Baron's stomach.

Squint opened the back of the jukebox and started working on the speed controls. When he turned it on, it was going faster than ever, and the painters started painting faster than ever. Finally, he found the right knob and slowed the music and the painters down. In a little while the room was painted, the newspaper was picked up, and the paint spills were mopped. They rolled the carpet back out again, brought up the pool table from the cellar, and assembled it in the transformed room. In a corner behind the furnace they found more of Claudius's things. There were five or six heavy wooden barstools, the end section of a curved and well-worn bar, two wall racks filled with pool cues, four brass spittoons, and a giant clock that was designed to hang from the ceiling on a chain like a pocket watch. In a box they found a picture of Claudius behind a bar, wearing an apron, and in the same picture frame was a single dollar bill, the kind of memento or traditional first dollar a businessman keeps forever. Among everything else Claudius had done, at one time, apparently, he had been the owner-operator of a billiard parlor.

All this equipment they hauled upstairs. When they were done, the living room was a room that would appeal to anybody. It wouldn't be right for a virtuous man, but it was right for them. There wasn't a high-rolling gambler or a lowlife bandit in Texas who wouldn't feel at home there, so it ought to feel right to Claudius when he came back.

In the late afternoon Panzer had them all stand around the pool table and pose for a picture.

They were congratulating themselves when there came from the kitchen a shriek, a scream that was almost human. Their teeth were on edge, the small hairs on the backs of their necks stood up. Suddenly bursting in from the kitchen came two terrified chickens with Herman right behind them, a meat cleaver in his hand.

One of the chickens circled the room, knocking against the walls like his head was already cut off, then flew right into the Mask's face. The other chicken flew behind the bar, and the Claw dived for it. They couldn't see what happened, but they didn't have to see to know. The Claw landed, and there was a loud, earsplitting GAWKKKKK. . . .

9: Fried Chicken

That night, cleaned of paint and all signs of painting except the splats and splashes on the Mask, some stuck with chicken feathers, the troupe of wrestlers and kids sat down to supper. Fried chickens, four fried chickens, in fact, filled their stomachs that evening. They had worked hard during the day, and a big meal was their reward. The Claw contributed as many bones to the pile as anyone, though every time he finished off a drumstick or a wing, he smiled sheepishly, delivering the bone to the pile with the attitude of a little boy asking for forgiveness.

"That's right," Rose chided him. "You ought to feel sorry, eating chicken like that. How do you know that drumstick's not off the poor thing you killed?"

"Herman mixed up the pieces," the Claw defended himself. "Besides, what difference does it make whether I eat it or you eat it? It's dead. Somebody's got to eat it."

"Don't make a bit of difference to me." She grinned. "I just thought it made a difference to you, killing something like that and eating it."

Herman frowned at them, and they let the conversation drop.

Betty looked at the Mask and told him, "Now you're gonna have to take it off, 'cause you gonna have to soak it in turpentine."

The Mask just smiled. There hadn't been a day in years that Betty hadn't tried in some way or another to get him to take off his mask. His feelings would have been hurt if she hadn't at least made an attempt.

"I might just keep it this way," he said. "It makes me look prettier."

In a way Squint couldn't believe it. He had lived and worked with the wrestlers in Claudius's troupe for two days, and a gentler bunch of people he'd never met before. What a monumental act it was for them to act mean and barbaric in the ring, he decided. The Claw *did* feel guilty for killing the chicken, and Squint had personally wrung the necks of hundreds of chickens, and it wasn't anything to feel guilty about; it was the way things were.

The thing that made it hard to believe was their size. Just looking at them made you want to be careful about what you said. There was a natural reluctance that kept you from getting too close; everything about them said watch out, yet you got the feeling being around them that it would be a lot easier to make them cry than make them mad. Squint wasn't even sure you could make them mad.

The telephone rang, and Julie went to answer it. They were finished eating and about to leave the table when Rose had an idea. "I know what let's do," she said. "Let's get dressed up in our outfits and show the kids." The kids had seen them in the ring, but they hadn't seen them in full costume.

Betty and Rose and the Baron and Panzer went up to their rooms to put on their costumes. It was the Mask's and Claw's night for the dishes, and they started clearing the table. Nobody told them to, they just got up and started doing it, and even Constance would have admired their breeding. "Why, what fine manners," she would have said. "You just don't know when someone's been raised in a good, Christian home."

Julie came back from the phone with a frown on her face. "It was the deacon," she said to Squint. "He wanted to make sure we had a ride to church tomorrow and were going and to let us know that we didn't have to expect him for dinner tomorrow—that is, not unless we wanted him."

Constance had been inviting the deacon to Sunday dinner for ten years, four years with Claudius at home and going on seven with him gone. If it hadn't been for Claudius's postcards, the Deacon would've tried to get him declared legally dead.

"And what did you tell him?" Squint asked Julie.

"That everything was changed now, and we weren't planning to go to his church anymore. I said it was my mother's church, not ours, and he ought not to plan on Sunday dinners anymore."

"Good girl," Squint told her. It's just what he would've said.

Outside, they heard the sound of a car driving up and a car door opening and slamming. Squint thought for a minute that it was Claudius coming back, but Julie shook her head no.

"It's Deacon Rambo," she said. "He was just calling from the gas station down the road."

10: The Deacon Gets Religion

For special occasions Deacon Rambo liked to dress in black. He never looked more strong and vigorous, Constance used to tell him, than when he wore black. As a result, he wore that color, or more properly, that lack of color, whenever he preached and whenever his religious duties took him to the Gainses' farm.

There had been few occasions in his life more important than the one at hand. For days now he'd been planning it. He'd had his suit cleaned and pressed, his long, thin black boots shined, and the black Buick Dyna-flo waxed and vacuumed. He had shaved extra close and talcumed his face, and he'd gone to the florist and bought, with his own money, a small wreath of bright red roses. What he hoped for was not to adopt the girl, though he was prepared to if that was all he could do; what he hoped for was to win her affection and marry her. She was seventeen years old, and that was old enough. He could, in fact, perform the ceremony himself, and in his coat pocket he carried the necessary marriage license. All he needed was for her to say yes and sign the license and get it witnessed.

The telephone call had almost destroyed him. Why had he called? he kept wondering and kicking himself in the brain. Why hadn't he just shown up at the door and given her the flowers, gotten her to say yes before she had the chance to say no?

Seeing the old school bus in the yard threw him. Something crazy was going on, and he didn't know what it was. What was an army-green school bus doing there?

He climbed the steps, crossed the porch, and, still looking at the bus, knocked on the door. When Squint opened the door and Deacon Rambo saw the living room, immediately he knew the answer. The pool table, the jukebox, the fan and the bar, the hideous moose head over the mantel where Constance's picture once hung. The deacon wasn't able to hide his shock and disappointment. "All my hopes and dreams . . . all my hopes and dreams," he kept saying. He sat down on one of the high-legged stools and hung his head between his knees. "He's come back. Just when I was so close, so close, he's come back." He covered the back of his head with his hands.

In the back of his mind he heard Squint talking to

him, the boy's voice coming like a whisper in a dark cave. "He needs a drink of water," the voice said.

There was another voice, an older voice, saying, "He doesn't have any blood in his head," that voice, too, coming from the cave. The cave was getting darker and darker and threatened to suffocate him. With the last of his energy, he lifted his head and opened his eyes, fully and hatefully expecting to see the face of Claudius Gains.

Standing in front of him, however, was something that took the breath out of his lungs so quickly that he could almost see it go. The Marked Marvel held out a glass of water for him to drink, but the deacon never saw it. All he saw was the black mask, the purple circles around the eyes, nose, and mouth, the ungodly chicken feathers sticking to the drops of white paint. The next thing he knew, or didn't know as the case may be, he was lying unconscious on the floor.

The poor deacon had no way of knowing that they meant him no harm. Just the opposite, in fact. They felt sorry for him and tried to make him more comfortable. The Mask took his arms, and the Claw his feet, and together they lifted him to the pool table and stretched him out. Julie got a pillow for his head, and Squint covered him with a sheet, unfortunately a dusty sheet from the cellar. The Marked Marvel took care of the wreath of roses; he didn't want them to get stepped on, so he placed them on the table near the deacon's feet. They were all concerned for his well-being, the Baron, Panzer, Betty, and Rose, and that is why they were standing behind the roses, waiting for him to regain consciousness.

The sight the deacon saw when he opened his eyes was completely innocent. There was the Baron, wearing a World War I flying helmet and goggles, a silk scarf around his neck. There was Panzer, a Gestapo cap on his head, a swastika hanging from his bare neck. There was Betty, wearing leopard-skin tights and dagger-sharp fingernails. Rose wore a simple two-foot-tall Marie Antoinette wig and a robe covered with sequined yellow flowers. The deacon didn't take it as innocent, however, and couldn't talk to ask them what they were doing. First he moaned; next he whimpered; then he threw off the sheet and ran for his life from the house.

Those inside heard him get in the car and start the engine, heard him kill it and start it again, and kill it and start it a third time before he got his nerves together enough to drive.

"Now what do you suppose caused that?" the Baron asked.

Squint was worried that they hadn't done as Claudius had asked and kept out of trouble.

They hadn't seen the last of Deacon Rambo; on that Squint was willing to bet.

11: Seymour

"I like it," Julie said. In the morning they had their first chance to enjoy the previous day and night's effort. Julie and Squint shot their first game of pool ever, taking almost two hours to play what is normally a thirty-minute game, finally learning how to hold the cues and where to aim, Julie winning with a short, straight shot on the fifteen ball to the side pocket.

"It's going to change our lives," she said, taking the cue from Squint's hand and handing it to the Mask, her next opponent. The room, save for the carpet, contained no traces of its former existence. Under Constance's hand it had been the equal of any parsonage parlor in Texas; under Claudius's spiritual guidance it'd been turned into a room where a person could feel at home.

Squint wasn't sure they needed the room changing their lives. He could count at least four major changes in the last week, starting with Constance's death on Sunday morning. But Julie was right in at least one respect: There were more major changes coming.

In the afternoon Squint sat on the front porch with Betty, Rose, and Herman and watched them shell peas.

He was there, of course, to watch for his father and so took notice of everything that passed on the road. He heard the motorcycle before he saw it. Even Betty,

Rose, and Herman, who weren't particularly alert to anything but their own pea picking, heard it coming down the road and watched.

"Sounds louder than the Germans," the Claw said, coming out on the porch as the motorcycle slowed down and turned in their road.

"Ain't got no muffler," Rose observed, stating what was obvious.

"What's that on the side?" the Baron asked. He had his monocle in, but he still couldn't make it out.

"It's a sidecar," Squint said. It was a sidecar.

"What in tarnation is in it?" Julie hollered, but nobody could tell. They had to wait for it to get up to the house before they could make it out.

Driving the motorcycle was what was plainly a human being, wearing a leather motorcycle coat and goggles. Riding in the sidecar was something that was plainly not human. Wearing its own goggles, waving at the people on the porch as the noisy contraption drove in front of the house, passed, circled around the parked truck and school bus, then returned to stop at the front steps was a bear, one of those trained circus bears.

The human being who was driving the machine mercifully shut off the engine and asked the crowd on the porch his question.

"Is this the Gains place?"

Squint didn't know what to do more than nod his head yes.

"Then you'd better move that bus and truck out of the way to the back," the driver said. "There's gonna be some big equipment coming in here tonight."

With that he started the engine again and drove off, leaving them tongue-tied and deaf.

"Now what do you suppose that was?" the Mask said, the noise of the motorcycle disappearing in the distance.

Panzer and the Baron moved the bus and truck and came back to the porch to wait with the others. It had to be Claudius's work, they all decided.

They waited, speculating on what it would be, and just before nightfall they heard the sound of the motorcycle coming back, this time followed by a wrecker truck with a crane on its back, two tractor-trailers with wild animals and the sign MC KAY BROTHERS CIRCUS in sun-bleached paint on the sides, one flatbed truck with a load under canvas, another one with a log-chained load of unidentifiable wooden structure material. Coming behind the convoy were six cars of workmen and Claudius in Panzer's green Chevy.

When everything was off the main road and moving toward the farm, Claudius zoomed past them and parked beside the house. Squint watched Claudius get out, wave, and start giving instructions to the truck drivers on where to go and what to do.

Then the motorcycle and sidecar stopped at the front steps again, and this time the driver and bear got out.

The driver came walking up to Squint and Julie first, taking off his goggles and handing Squint his business card. "Colonel McKay Brothers here," he said, turning to shake hands with Panzer and the Baron, the Mask and the Claw. The women and Herman took the peas inside as they were beginning to gather too much dust. "Formerly of McKay Brothers Circus, now defunct," Brothers went on, "and this here"—he indicated the bear—"is Seymour."

With that, Brothers reached into his leather coat and pulled out a pint bottle of whiskey and took a hard slosh. He made a quick, halfhearted offer of the bottle to the men, then screwed the top back on and had it back in his pocket before they could accept. "Seymour's thirsty," he said. "Could somebody here get him a bucket of water?"

Seymour gave a low growl, and Brothers looked at him. "He'd rather have some iced tea if you got it," he said.

Seymour followed Squint and Julie to the kitchen.

"Great living room," Brothers said, following them all. Herman was used to strange things in his kitchen, and a bear was nothing more to him than a big dog.

He took a pitcher of tea from the refrigerator and looked around for a large pot.

"Just let him have the pitcher," Brothers said. "He'll be fine."

Herman reluctantly handed the bear the pitcher, and Seymour took it in both paws and drained it like it was honey. What the bear accidentally spilled on his stomach, he licked off; then he opened the screen door to the back porch with his paw and went out. He looked around for a few moments, decided on the shady end of the porch, lay down, and went to sleep.

12: The Fountain of Money

Claudius didn't offer them any explanations on what he was doing, and Squint didn't ask for any. Squint himself never could stand being interrupted with dumb questions—What are you doing? Why are you doing it? Wouldn't it be better if you did it this way? A person ought to be able to see what was going on with his own two eyes and figure it out with his own brain.

The first four things off the trucks looked like gigantic desks. They were easily as big as a full-sized room once they were set in place on the ground and a crew of men bolted them together. Squint watched from the porch and figured out that it was some kind of stage.

The rest of the men were working like an army of rabbits, laying out sections of bleachers. Claudius was working with them in a supervisory position, showing them where he wanted what, arranging the bleachers around the stage. He laid out two sections on each side, each section seating, Squint figured, three hundred people, twenty across and fifteen rows high. Before it got dark, Squint watched his father plan two more full sections and one corner. By Squint's count, Claudius was planning to show whatever he was going to show onstage to about eighteen hundred people.

After it got dark, the men turned their car and truck lights on the area where they were working. Squint watched them build the bleachers for a while from his bedroom, then fell asleep.

There was someone else watching the activities that night. Through a pair of dime-store opera glasses, Deacon Lawrence Rambo studied the construction, or what he could see of it, from the road. He sat in his car, safely off the Gains property, and kept notes with the stub of a broken pencil and the back of an offering envelope, evidence in case he needed it. On the back of the envelope he had written, "Monsters," "Masks," "Bears," "Claws for hands," and "Criminals." Wondering what the wooden bleachers were and unable to tell from such a distance, he wrote the word "Cages" and put a question mark after it.

Shortly before midnight the Deacon grew weary of his intelligence gathering and started his car and slipped away. Had he stayed a few minutes longer, he would have seen the first section of wall go up, a highway billboard with the message SEE ROCK CITY in six-foot red letters facing the road.

A fountain, Claudius had promised, a fountain of money to save the farm and quench their financial thirsts forever. In the morning Squint looked out his bedroom window on the night's accomplishment.

It was an arena, a wrestling arena. In the center was the ring, the posts and ropes in place, the floor of it covered with a canvas mat. Around the ring on all sides except the house side were the bleacher seats, rising from the ringside aisle to near the top of the billboard walls. The billboard walls ran from both sides of the front of the house to the opposite side of the arena, where a gap for the entrance was. For a front gate, the swinging doors from the barn had been installed.

13: Claudius Reveals His Plan

Claudius was tired, but happy. He tested the water coming from the sink faucet to see that it was warm enough, then filled a broiling pan with hot water and set it in the center of the kitchen floor. He pulled up a chair, took off his shoes and socks, rolled up his pants legs, and started soaking his feet.

McKay Brothers sat at the kitchen table and worked up a contract.

"I, Claudius H. Gains, do hereby agree to pay Colonel McKay Brothers, my good friend, the sum of one dollar a day rental on one wrestling ring and equipment, two thousand general admission seating, and eight standard advertising billboards. The period of rental is no less than two weeks, from June 19, 1951, to July 3, 1951, after which time I, Claudius H. Gains, agree to purchase the above said equipment at a cost of seven hundred and fifty dollars—"

"Five hundred," Claudius said.

"—Six hundred dollars . . . and further, I agree to take the bear known as Seymour, house him and feed him, and teach him to wrestle."

Squint came downstairs to the kitchen and heard Brothers reading the last part of the contract and looked on as the colonel gave it to Claudius to sign.

"We're going to put on wrestling matches in our front yard?"

His father pulled one steaming pink foot from the water, let it cool, then eased it back in and cooled the other one. "From now on, it's gonna be known as the Gains Arena and Wrestling Academy," Claudius said.

Brothers was doing the mathematics, figuring in his notebook. "Two thousand seats—at how much a seat?"

"A dollar and a quarter for adults, fifty cents for kids under twelve, all babies in laps free."

"A dollar twenty-five times one thousand, seven hundred. Fifty cents times one hundred . . ." He multiplied the figures. "You're going to have to just about sell out for three nights in a row to pay the bank."

Claudius had worked out the figures in his head long before he'd gone to Dallas to find Brothers. "And that doesn't give me much to pay the wrestlers," he said. "Fortunately I know some wrestlers who ought to be willing to sacrifice." He thought about it and smiled. "Including one overage, overweight bear."

Panzer and the Baron came in, poured coffee, and sat at the table and listened. "There's Ranger Ralph Travis and his partner," Panzer offered. "They owe us a favor."

"Right," Claudius remembered, "right."

"So all we need now is fans with money," the Baron said, putting a bit of a damper on the excitement that was building. Raising $6,000 in three days was a problem that was real.

Claudius dried his feet and put his shoes and socks back on. "I'm just going to have to come up with something," he said. "I thought up the first idea, and I'll think of the next." He lifted the pan of water and carried it to the sink. Then he opened the refrigerator and took out a six-pack of cold beer and glanced out the window at his chair. "No," he hollered. "I won't have it!" And he grabbed the broom and started on a run through the screen door and back porch.

Seymour was sitting in Claudius's chair, peacefully shaded by the umbrella, his feet up, contentedly staring at the bouncing beer lights, which he had somehow managed to turn on. Claudius whopped the back of the chair with the broom, scaring the poor bear out of his reverie, and chased him halfway to the house.

If Seymour could have talked, he would probably have been cussing. He opened the door to the kitchen by bumping it with his paw and catching it before it closed with his snout. Herman felt sorry for him and gave him a big bowl of peach ice cream to eat.

Claudius was in his chair, a beer in his hand, thinking.

14: The Road to Waterloo . . .

When Squint, later in the day, looked out and saw the sun peeping under the umbrella and shining on Claudius's head, he suspected that Claudius was doing more sleeping than thinking and went out to see what he could do. If nothing else, he could swing the chair around so Claudius wouldn't wake up with a cooked head.

True enough, his father was sleeping. And dreaming of something masterful, judging from the expression on his face, which bore a striking similarity to Napoleon's above him. Also like the picture, Claudius had his right hand tucked between the buttons on his chest; it would be a sin to let such a great mind cook.

Squint turned the chair, and his father woke up. "I need a calendar," Claudius said.

15: . . . Is Paved with the Best-Laid Schemes

"Okay," he said, "today is Monday. I want Panzer and the Baron to take a run to town and buy enough big lights to light this place." Claudius had gathered the troupe on the front porch and was pointing out things that had to be done. "Run the wire along the top of the wall, and give me three lights on each section, two pointing at the ring and one on the seats so some old lady won't slide through the slats and kill herself. Give me one on both sides of the gate and one on both sides of the porch."

"I got some lights at my place in Dallas you can

have," Brothers said. "You can string a cable across the top and hang them over the ring."

Claudius nodded and went on. "Okay, Tuesday and Wednesday we work up a new act, and you two, Mask and Claw, you work with Seymour and see what he can do. Thursday, we go to Dallas and wrestle at the Legion. Friday, we pick up McKay's lights and come back—"

"You still ain't said how we're gonna get two thousand people in here," Betty reminded him.

"I'm getting to it. I'm getting to it." Claudius was a man who got impatient when he was interrupted. "We come back from Dallas, and we've got money again. We still got part of Friday, Saturday, Sunday, and Monday to stock up a concession stand. Herman, you and Julie will be in charge of concessions. I'll promote the matches."

Claudius held up the calendar and showed them three circled days. "Next Tuesday, Wednesday, and Thursday nights, the twenty-seventh, twenty-eighth, and twenty-ninth, we hold our grand opening tournament."

That left the wrestlers a bit confused.

"See, I announce you six wrestlers as the faculty of the wrestling academy. The purpose of the tournament is to find out which one of you is going to be the head-boss teacher, so you wrestle each other to decide. Then,

on the third night, I award the winner with a prize of
ten thousand dollars cash, and the winner challenges
anybody in the audience to wrestle him for the money."

"What if somebody does?" Panzer asked. He wasn't
overly thrilled with the idea of wrestling some big hod
from the oil fields who could move five-hundred-pound
pipes like they were made of balsa wood.

"Somebody will," Claudius told them. That was the
crowning feature of his plan. He looked at Herman.
"Herman will challenge and win. He wins the money,
which goes to pay the bank the next morning, and he
wins a scholarship to the Gains Internationally Famous
College of Wrestling, the Birthplace of World Champions."

Of course, they had to think about it. A lot of details
had to be worked out, such as who was to wrestle who
and what kind of show they were going to put on. But
all through the discussions they kept the big things in
mind. The main point of what they were doing was to
get the money and pay off the goons at the bank. At
some time or another all of them had suffered from
dealing with banks.

"Don't worry about the people," Claudius kept telling them. "I'll bring 'em in for the first match; it's up
to all of us to bring 'em back for the second and third."

"I tried to borrow money on a diamond ring once,"
the Claw recalled. Everybody spent the evening in the

arena, puttering around with small tasks, installing the ring bell, spreading sawdust where they expected the most traffic, talking among themselves. "Not for a girl," the Claw went on, "but for myself. I figured if I had a big diamond ring on my hand, people wouldn't notice the hook so much."

"A person can't wrestle forever," Panzer was saying. "Me and the Baron, old Betty and Rose, we ain't no spring chickens anymore."

Squint moved in and out among them, helping where there was something to do.

"So I go to the bank and tell them what I want and what I do for a living. 'I'm a wrestler,' I say, and they look at the hook and start laughing."

Panzer said, "A couple of years ago the Baron and I go to a bank. We want to borrow some money for a farm like this, some place where we can rest in our old age, play with our grandchildren." Panzer had a sad look in his eyes, sad and determined. "They just looked at us and made up their minds no."

Squint came to the conclusion that saving the farm meant more to the people who didn't own it than it did to him and Julie.

McKay Brothers had brought something else with him when his men delivered the arena, and that night he set it up in the living room, a little Brownie home movie projector and a screen. Claudius passed out cans of beer to all the wrestlers, and they, Squint, Julie, and Herman found seats around the pool table for the viewing. Brothers took a drink of whiskey from his pocket flask and loaded the film.

The film was made of short clips taken of his circus when circuses were still profitable to take on the road. Brothers's circus had only been one ring, but it had featured everything the big ones did, elephants, a lion-tamer act, highfliers, acrobats, fancy riders and ropers, and clowns. In one sequence the clowns played a base-ball game. The clown who was batting hit the ball so hard it exploded, and he took off wobbling in his three-foot-long shoes to first base. The clown playing be-tween second and third peeled a banana and placed it down carefully in the base path. A rhubarb began when the clown stepped on the peel and slipped down. All the clowns piled up on each other except one who got the banana peel, dipped it in a bucket of water, and poured the water on the pile of clowns. All of a sudden nobody could stand up. The banana peel had made the water so slick that they couldn't even stay on their hands and knees without flopping on their bellies.

Brothers told stories about the circus and how it was in the old days. "Everybody who had anything to do with the circus filled in for everybody else when they had to. This next little bit shows our road manager filling in for the human cannonball who had the flu," he explained. The reluctant road manager is a younger, thinner Claudius Gains.

They just about have to drag him to the ladder and prod him up it with a stick. He goes up, though, adjusts his helmet and glasses, and waves at the crowd. The cannon looks big enough to send Claudius to the moon, at least a lot farther than the net at the far end of the tent.

Just as the lanyard is pulled and smoke from the cannon begins to fill the screen, the film flickered once and ran out. Everybody groaned except Claudius and Brothers, who started laughing.

"Now you know how I got my medal," Claudius told them.

A pool shark, a manager for a girls' softball team, a soldier in the war, the road manager for a circus, a farmer (if you counted the years he lived with Constance), a wrestling manager . . . Squint went to bed that night thinking that there wasn't nothing his father couldn't do.

With only Seymour for a witness, Claudius was up late into the night, pacing the floor around the pool table, sinking an occasional ball with ease, thinking of ways to make sure they got a crowd, trying to think of anything he might have overlooked.

16: The Preacher and the Bear

The next day there began the first in a series of problems. Squint was working the splinter patrol near the top seats on the side of the arena above the gate. His duty was to feel along where people would sit with his hand and, where it felt rough, to run a hand plane or sandpaper over it. The old wooden bleachers hadn't been used in ten years, and it was better to get rid of splinters the slow way than to have a customer discover them the painful way. He heard cars slow down on the main road and looked over the wall to see the sheriff's and deacon's cars turn into their property. If it wasn't a problem starting, it certainly had all the makings of one.

Now the sheriff wasn't exactly a popular man in the county; it was rumored, among other things, that he was crookeder than snake guts. Still, he'd never been caught, and he got reelected for term after term by arresting people only when they had to be arrested, when they were so wild and crazy nothing else would do, and by giving and receiving favors instead of money. A poor man could give just as good a favor as a rich man, both votes were counted equal, and the sword of justice was blind.

Squint watched them coming through the dust and ran to the house to warn Claudius.

The sheriff and the deacon took time to look at the walls of the arena. To the left of the main gate was the SEE ROCK CITY sign; to the right was the picture of a matronly woman in a tight corset, advertising Nature's Aid Foundation Garments.

"See there," the deacon was saying, "if they're not practicing witchcraft in there, how come they need these walls?"

"Witchcraft doesn't happen to be against the law, Deacon," the sheriff had to remind him. The sheriff wasn't a big man, no more than five and a half feet tall. He looked even shorter than that because he wore his khaki uniform pants legs inside his high-topped boots, and the hogleg pistol he carried on his side hung down to the middle of his knee. To make him look even less like a lawman, he had a potbelly and wore thick, owlish-looking glasses. Still, he knew the law, and witchcraft wasn't a crime. Not only was it not a crime, but a man was a fool to make a witch mad at him. His uncle had made that mistake once and woke up the next morning with the world's biggest boil on the end of his nose.

Posted on the garage-door gate was a sign that said BILLBOARD SPACE FOR RENT—INQUIRE WITHIN, CLAUDIUS GAINS.

Squint had to tell Claudius about them scaring the deacon half to death, as that was probably the reason for his fetching out the sheriff.

Claudius frowned his disapproval, saying, "You don't go making people mad at you. You get enough enemies by accident. There's no gain in making them on purpose."

"Take Me Back to Tulsa, I'm Too Young to Marry" was playing on the jukebox.

"Not appropriate," Claudius said, and unplugged it. "Is Burl Jernigen still the sheriff?" Claudius asked. Squint, sorry for making the mistake, though it really hadn't been his fault, nodded yes. Claudius quickly rummaged in a drawer behind the bar, smiled, and came up holding a small gold object, which he pinned to the lapel of his coat. It was a moose head, the emblem of the Loyal Order of the Fraternity of Moose. When Claudius owned his pool hall, he'd found it convenient to be a member of many clubs: the Moose, Lions, Elks, Grizzlies, and Longhorn Boosters. He didn't belong, but he also had the service pins for the Rotary, KCs, KLs, and Kiwanis.

The sheriff, Burl Jernigen, wore two things on his shirt: his badge and a little moose head pin. When he walked across the arena, and Claudius came down the porch steps to meet him, the first thing they did was smile and shake hands.

"Well, Claudius," the sheriff said, "people in these parts thought you were gone forever."

"Nobody's ever gone forever, Brother Burl. We're like what those Chinese fellows say; we just keep reincarnating."

The deacon didn't like seeing the sheriff and Claudius so friendly. "Arrest him, Sheriff," Rambo said. "You just heard the words out of his own mouth. They're out here practicing reincarnation."

Things were set for a showdown between Claudius and the deacon, a showdown that Squint felt responsible for and the sheriff would have to handle. At that moment, however, Seymour, who had been sleeping under the front porch, came crawling out and started sniffing the deacon's leg. The deacon went white and tried to hide behind Sheriff Burl. Seymour must have found an interesting smell on the deacon's leg because he kept trying to get to it.

"Use your gun!" the deacon hollered at the sheriff. "For God's sake, man, use your gun!"

The sheriff, he wasn't sure about the bear. He didn't like being between the two, but it wouldn't look good to voters for their sheriff to let somebody get eaten by a bear. "Can you call this critter off?" he asked Claudius.

Claudius calmly told Seymour, "Seymour, let the man alone." The bear pulled back. "Now go inside," Claudius said, and Seymour went up the steps, bumped the screen door with his paw, and went inside. He didn't go very far inside, however. He sat there watching the deacon, and the deacon stood there watching him.

"Uh, Deacon," the sheriff said, "my procedures say I've got to interview this witness in private. You don't mind waiting in the car, do you?"

The deacon didn't mind, and when he was gone, Claudius and Sheriff Burl threw their arms around each other and started laughing.

"I could use a bear like that in my reelection campaign," the sheriff said.

"Can't let you have him for a while," Claudius said, "but there's other ways to help." They went inside and sat at the bar and drank some beer together, talking about old times and the wrestling matches Claudius was planning to put on. With the deacon out there sweating in his hot car, Claudius and the sheriff worked out a deal. The sheriff had refereed prizefights in his younger days, and he didn't imagine wrestling would be that much different. Claudius had himself a referee for the matches, and the sheriff had himself some good publicity and a billboard. Where it said SEE ROCK CITY, as soon as a crew could get out and do it, a new sign would say REELECT SHERIFF BURL JERNIGEN, A FEARLESS MAN, AND FAIR.

When the sheriff and the deacon were gone, the sheriff having explained that he couldn't arrest anybody unless they broke the law, things got back on schedule. "That's the kind of problem we need more of," Claudius said, and Squint didn't feel so bad.

17: A Fearless Bear

"You've just got to hold still," Betty was saying. Later in the day the wrestlers started working out their routines for the trip to Dallas. Betty and Rose had gotten an idea and taken one of Constance's red and white checkered tablecloths. They'd made Seymour a pair of wrestling trunks and were trying to get them on him. They had one of his legs in the trunks, and while Rose was holding him down on his back, Betty was trying to get the other leg in. "Hold still, I tell you," Betty said, grabbing his big toe and shaking it.

She got the second leg in, and they let him up. Getting up was a mistake on the bear's part because as soon as he got to his all fours, Betty was on him, scooting the trunks up his midsection. Rose had him by the nose to keep him from going anywhere while Betty got the straps over his shoulders and buttoned them in back.

"Now stand up," Rose said.

By that time Seymour was willing to do anything the two women told him to do. All he wanted was to

get away before they thought of something else. He
stood up in his checkered trunks, feeling like some
dern fool teddy bear. The trunks were more like a
sunsuit than regular wrestling trunks.

Betty said, "Ah."

Rose said, "Beautiful."

And Seymour ran from the room.

18: Claudius at Work

Claudius spent a good part of the day on the telephone, arranging credit in town, ordering things like
tickets, and calling person to person all over the state
of Texas, looking for Ranger Ralph and Hog Jarvis.
When he finally got Ranger Ralph on the phone, Ralph
was in Del Rio, half the state away, and wasn't in any
mood to repay favors.

"You won't believe how hot it is down here," the
Ranger told him. "I'm laying in bed. I've got the bed
moved over to the air conditioner. I've got a bag of
ice on my stomach and the fan blowing on my feet.
I ain't about to drive five hundred miles to wrestle for
free. I just opened a beer, and I ain't gonna leave this
room."

"Sounds like you're real comfortable," Claudius
said.

"First time in days I've been comfortable," the Ranger said.

Claudius pictured him in bed, out of his rhinestone-studded shirt, out of his butterfly slick leather boots, out of the corset he wore to hide his beer belly from his adoring public. Claudius had met many a wrestler in his years, but he'd never met one more vain than Ranger Ralph Travis. "Sounds like you're so comfortable down there you've forgotten who rescued you from that doghouse in Hot Springs and taught you to wrestle. . . ."

Squint came through the hall and overheard Claudius at work.

"Today is Wednesday," his father said. "You and the Hog are on next Wednesday night." Claudius held the telephone away from his ear for a few moments. Squint could hear the loud complaining coming from the other end, and when it subsided, Claudius said, "Good, I'm expecting you," and hung up.

"A problem?" Squint said.

"It's the same old universal problem," Claudius said, looking up another telephone number in the local directory. "How do you get somebody to do something they don't want to do?"

"How do you do it?"

"You just remind them that happiness is a two-edged sword," Claudius said. "Somebody gives it to you, you give it back to them."

When Squint thought about his father's words for a while, they still didn't make any sense.

19: Doing the Bear Dance

Herman sat on the front porch with an ice-cream maker between his legs in front of him. He dumped in a bowl of fresh-cut strawberries and started churning. Squint sat down next to him on the steps and watched what was happening in the ring.

In the ring, Panzer and the Baron were trying to teach Seymour to wrestle, but all he wanted to do was hug and dance. Panzer tried to rough him up the way kids rough up a puppy; the bear took that kind of play the way a sad old hound dog does, by rolling his eyes and yawning. The three of them together looked like the losers of a dance contest, tired and ready for bed.

Brothers, sitting at ringside, closed his eyes and shook his head. The Mask and Claw took over with the same results. Without the spark of understanding that would have made him as human as everybody else, Seymour was doing what he thought they wanted him to do, dancing with them. Brothers stopped the act by ringing the bell and called Seymour to him. He waved the four wrestlers back, opened his tunic, and took out his flask. He opened the top and handed it to the bear and said, "Drink." That was no problem. In two gulps the flask was empty. "Now sic 'em," Brothers ordered.

That's what Seymour needed, a shot of rotgut whiskey and instructions he could understand. He got down on his all-fours and charged the Masked Marvel like a bull. The Mask saw it coming and jumped clear. The Baron and Panzer weren't so quick or so fortunate. The Baron's monocle went flying one way, and the Baron the other. Panzer flipped end over end and came down on his back. The Claw was standing in the corner at the time and climbed the ropes to safety as the bear cut under him and headed back to the center of the ring.

"Now show 'em your stuff!" Brothers yelled, and Seymour reared back on his hind legs and did the bear dance. If you could have seen him, you'd have sworn he was laughing.

The Claw and the Mask got their senses together first and were out of the ring. The Baron and Panzer were in the process of regaining theirs when Brothers yelled, "Sic 'em again!" The bear came down and took a running start at them, but by then they were diving headfirst through the ropes.

"Not bad," Claudius said. He'd come out to stand on the porch and see the last act. "Good!" he yelled to his wrestlers. "We'll use it."

20: Claudius Tells a Story

"It's got to be written somewhere," Claudius said, shooting the cue ball to strike the nine ball to hit two rails and sink the fifteen ball in one of the end pockets and thereby earning fifteen points. "It's got to be written that the man who gambles is just as doomed as the man who doesn't gamble. That's what makes people gamble. They figure, Suppose I lose. Okay, I lose. Everybody loses anyway. At least I had a chance to win."

He shot the nine ball again, causing it to strike the rail quickly and bounce back against the cue ball, sending the cue ball back sharply to strike the fourteen ball and dump it in the side pocket. ". . . which is why there will always be somebody around to take their money."

He then shot the nine, ten, eleven, twelve, and thirteen balls with straight shots into the pockets. He'd made the one through seven, left the eight hanging in the pocket for Brothers (his only mistake), and run the rest. He looked at the table fondly and said, "I used to earn a pretty good living on this old table . . . till I was forced into retirement."

Everybody except the Mask and Julie, who were sitting in the porch swing and watching through the window, was in the living room to see Claudius demonstrate his skill at hustling pool. They'd worked and practiced hard that day and were in a Texas beer-sipping, lighting-up-a-cigar mood. "Tell 'em how you got forced into retirement," Brothers said. "I ain't heard that story in years."

It was a storytelling mood, not really arrived at by accident on Claudius's part. It was a duty to tell your story to your son and daughter, so he opened a beer and sat on one of the high-legged barstools.

"There was a guy come through town, and this was back in the old days, looked like they'd just invented shoes the day before he put his on. He came in and started shooting pool on this table." Claudius got up and patted the table with his hand.

"Back in those days, you got to understand, there wasn't a straight cue in Tyler. Nor a straight table. You had to shoot with things that were bowed like bananas on tables that had patches on them, and the balls themselves had hunks broke in the sides from them hod-carrying would-be cowboys bouncing them around the room. This was the only table worth shooting on."

Everybody, especially Squint, looked at the table.

"This table was reserved for serious gambling—though no gambling was supposed to be allowed. I had a sign on the wall to that effect. I kept the table covered, except for important occasions.

"I had a little sign that I used to keep on the table. Since there was no gambling allowed by law, the sign said IT COSTS $25 A GAME TO PLAY ON THIS TABLE—SEE CLAUDIUS GAINS, MANAGER.

"His shoes squeaked, his suit looked like it just came off a dummy, and when he took his coat off, he was wearing bright yellow suspenders. I walked over to him to tell him he couldn't shoot on *this* table.

"He said, 'Get yourself a cue. I'll play you for it.' I shot him for it, and he won."

There had to be more to the story than just that. Everybody, including Brothers, who hadn't heard the story in this particular way of telling, was waiting to know what happened.

"He was better than me," Claudius said, shrugging. "He won the flip and broke. He ran a game of billiards on me and beat me before I knew what was happening, walking around the table in those shoes, snapping his suspenders, shooting with a crooked cue on my own table. He made shots that you'd have thought were impossible to make."

Claudius walked around the table and shot the cue ball hard and straight against a distant rail. On the table by itself, it bounced off five more rails and fell in the corner pocket. He got it out, put it back where it had been, bounced it off the same six rails, and sank it in the same pocket.

"I said, 'How much money you got with you?' His

shoes, his hayseed suit and suspenders—they didn't fool me for a minute. He was a shooter from someplace big, and he took out a wad of bills. I didn't have near that kind of money, so I put up the pool hall against a thousand dollars, played another game and won, I think by about two balls. I had a thousand dollars of his money . . . pure luck.

"And then it suddenly occurred to me that there I was, running a pool hall that I'd won anyway, with a thousand dollars in my pocket, thirty years old and wasting away—and here was somebody who wanted to take over all my troubles."

Claudius looked around the room. "I told him that there wasn't any use our shooting anymore; I'd keep the table, the thousand dollars, the stuff I wanted from the building I could take with me, and I signed everything over to him, right then and there, and got married, and became a farmer." He looked at Squint. "And a father," he added.

The Masked Marvel and Julie weren't in the swing anymore. Claudius was aware that the swing wasn't squeaking on its chains, and he walked over to the screen door and looked outside to see them holding hands and looking at the moon.

"The way you told it the first time," Brothers said, taking a swig out of his flask, "you got skinned."

"Yeah," Claudius said, considering what he was looking at, "you might say I got skinned."

21: The Next Three Days

The next three days went quickly, with events taking place on or nearly on Claudius's schedule. On Thursday, exactly one week after Squint and Julie had discovered their father at the American Legion Arena in Dallas, Claudius loaded his wrestlers, Brothers, and Seymour on the bus and took them back to Dallas for their return exhibition. Herman fixed them a picnic basket of fifty sliced turkey sandwiches, three gallons of potato salad, which the wrestlers ate on the way to keep it from spoiling, and a half bushel basket of mixed fruit. They stayed the night in Dallas so they could get the lights Brothers had promised them. Squint, Julie, and Herman remained on the farm, Squint reading wrestling magazines to learn more about the sport, Julie mooning over the Masked Marvel like one of those war widows in the movies. She spent more time in front of the mirror primping than she'd ever spent before, and when Squint kidded her about it, she wouldn't kid back. Mostly she ignored him or called him a child.

On Friday, exactly one week after Claudius and his wrestlers had first come to live at the farm, the old bus came limping back.

Squint and Julie were sitting in the kitchen when Seymour came up on the back porch, opened the screen door, and walked in. He went to Herman and showed Herman his front paw, which was hurt and wrapped with a bandage. Squint and Julie went out to the bus to find out what had happened and help unload stuff. The Baron had a lump on his head that would have won the Grand Lump Award at any county fair. There was a two-inch-square plug missing in the back of the Masked Marvel's mask, revealing a lock of blond, curly hair. Claudius was the only one smiling. Squint asked what happened, and the Baron glared and pointed in the direction of the house.

"I'll tell you what happened," he said. "That bear went crazy and just about did us in. If he hadn't stepped on the Claw's hook and hurt himself, I don't know what would've happened."

"Aw, nothing happened," Claudius said, dismissing the whole adventure. Under his arm he had a stack of posters he'd had printed in Dallas. The posters had pictures of all the wrestlers in a circle around a drawing of the arena. "The Constance M. Gains Memorial Arena," it said under the drawing. It looked more like an aerial view of the Cotton Bowl than anything else; the porch in the drawing resembled a Roman temple. "Looks kinda nice, don't it?" Claudius said.

On Saturday everybody worked together to hang the lights over the ring. On Saturday night, with but three full days between them and the first of the matches and but six days between them and eviction by the bank, Claudius took the wrestlers to Tyler, where they were interviewed on radio.

22: The Durwood Henry Show

Durwood Henry was twenty-one years old and still wore the acne of his teenage years on his long, skinny face. His neck was dangerously thin, like it was made out of one of those skinlike miracle plastic substances they use on dolls and had been stretched too far for comfort. He wore a long-sleeved nylon sport shirt, the pastel kind you could see through, only he didn't wear anything under it. Radio announcing was definitely the wrong profession for him for the time being because his voice was still cracking.

Durwood sat behind the console in the broadcast studio of station KRIT, which the disc jockeys called K-Right and the dedicated listeners called K-Rat. Seated beside him so as to be able to share the same microphone was Claudius. Against the glass wall of the studio, in folding chairs, sat the wrestlers. Durwood punched buttons on the console when the second hand on the wall clock swept across the top to make the time exactly six-thirty. His show began with his theme song, "Under the Double Eagle," the introduction, "It's the Durwood Henry Show, with your host,

Durwood Henry!" and the sponsor's message, "Brought to you by those fine folks who make Sammy's Cream, now with chlorophyll, who want to remind you that athletes' foot fungus can be mighty mean, and if your cream's not green, your toes're not clean."

That commercial, among others, was the reason listeners called the station Rat Radio.

"A sign on the wall lit up the words ON THE AIR, and Durwood Henry commenced announcing.

"Hello, ladies and gentlemen and sports fans everywhere. This is Durwood Henry, and seated in the studio with me tonight is a bunch of people I really wish you could be here to see. There's one man who's wearing a black and purple mask on his head; there's another man with a meat hook instead of a hand; there's one who's in a panzer tank driver's outfit; there's a woman wearing a leopard-skin bathing suit, and another woman wearing Marie Antoinette the Fourteenth hair. And you won't believe this, but sitting in a chair right here in front of me, wearing a red and white checkered playsuit and straw hat, is a real, live bear."

"That's not really a playsuit, Durwood." Claudius leaned over and cut in. "That's a pair of old-fashioned wrestling trunks, the kind they used to wear in the 1880s."

"That *is* a real bear. . . . It isn't just somebody dressed up in a bear suit?"

"No, it's a real bear. You'll notice he's got a bandage

on his paw. That's because a couple of nights ago, when he was wrestling in Dallas, he accidentally stepped on the Steel Claw's steel claw and had to disqualify himself in the third fall."

"I'm talking to Colonel Claudius Gains, a former resident of Tyler who many in the listening audience will remember as the owner and operator of the Gains Recreation Center. There's probably a lot of you listening who learned your first lessons in pool in Gains's establishment. Now it turns out that Colonel Gains is the manager of a group of professional wrestlers, the group in the studio tonight. Tell us, Colonel, what brings you back to this neck of the piney woods?"

"Money," Claudius said.

Squint, Julie, and Herman were listening with Brothers to the little radio in the middle of the kitchen table. "One thing you can always say about Claudius," Brothers remarked, "he doesn't beat around bushes."

"Money?" Durwood asked.

"That's right, money," Claudius went on. "I got so much of it lately I've come back to Tyler to give some of it away. To bring your listeners up-to-date, they no longer have to drive all over Texas or all the way to Bossier City to see good professional wrestling; I've opened a new arena right here in the Tyler area, just two miles south of town on Route Three. In addition to the arena, I'm announcing the opening of the Claudius Gains College of Wrestling, the Home of Future World Champions."

"You mentioned something about giving away money. I'm sure the folks at home want to hear about that."

"My pleasure," Claudius said. "My pleasure. First of all, look at the Baron and Panzer there. They're going into their thirtieth year as professional wrestlers, and so are Badlands Betty and Rose of Texas. That's one hundred and twenty years of ring experience, and I couldn't begin to list the awards and prizes they've won over the years. Over the last five years they've been teaching my young wrestlers, the Masked Marvel and the Steel Claw, decorated heroes of the German war, to be champion wrestlers, to put that wartime courage to work in peacetime, so to speak. Now the Mask and the Claw are so good I'm holding a grand elimination contest to find out which one of the six is the best since, as you know, every wrestling college needs a grand champion."

"Uh, we'll be right back to find out where the money comes in after these messages," Durwood announced, and pushed a button.

"That man could talk the skin right off a snake," Brothers said. The messages were for Sammy's Cream, Sammy's Powder, and Sammy's Medicated Nasal Spray.

Then, "We're back," Durwood said, and the interview continued. "How much are you going to give away, Colonel, and to who?"

"This coming Tuesday night, after Badlands Betty and the Rose of Texas have it out to see who's the boss of the women's division, the two youngsters are going to go at each other. The next night, after a preliminary bout between Ranger Ralph Travis and Hog Jarvis—that's this coming Wednesday night for those of you who plan to pass up prayer meeting for something more exciting—the Baron and Panzer Kaufman will be matched against each other. They'll be fighting for their honor, so you know it's gonna be rough. Then, on Thursday night, the winning wrestler from Tuesday will meet the winner from Wednesday night; it'll be the best of the young and strong against the best of the old and experienced for the college championship, so get your tickets early. Now for the money . . ."

"Yes, the money," Durwood echoed.

"I'm putting up a cash prize of ten thousand dollars of my own money that says no matter who our champion is, he'll be able to beat anyone in the audience. If there's anybody out there who's got courage enough to get in the ring with our champion and beat him in regular wrestling, that man will get the ten thousand. I'll be there to give it to him."

"Ten thousand dollars," Durwood said, wobbling his head around on his neck like the famous balanced rock. "I don't think I've ever seen ten thousand dollars."

"And tomorrow, Sunday, at one P.M., we're having an open house for the press and all wrestling fans, where my wrestlers and Seymour the Wrestling Bear will be available for autographs and interviews. Refreshments will be sold, and tickets will go on sale; advance prices are a dollar and a quarter for adults, fifty cents for children under twelve. Tickets at the gate on Tuesday, Wednesday, and Thursday will be a dollar thirty-five and sixty cents. Come one, come all."

For ten grand, Durwood told the audience, he'd almost be tempted to risk his own neck. If Sammy's Cream would agree to it, he'd be there to broadcast the matches. Live from ringside.

23: The Angel of Sorrow

Homemade cookies and Kool-Aid were put on the side of the ring facing the front porch for the newsmen and guests who would be arriving soon. Strips of crepe paper were strung around the arena. Red, white, and blue, they hung from the roof of the porch, on the corner posts of the ring, from the tops of the billboard walls, from the lights, and from the open barn-door gate. Claudius had borrowed two flags from the local American Legion, the flag of the United States and the flag of Texas, and both hung at angles from their staffs mounted on the posts on either side of the front-porch steps. The added color given to the arena did much to hide the makeshift quality of the structure. A blue ribbon stretched across the main gate. Claudius carried a pair of scissors in his coat pocket for the cutting.

The wrestlers and Seymour were in costume, and shortly before one o'clock Claudius marched them across the arena to form a reception line outside the main gate. Herman carried a roll of tickets, and Julie carried a money box.

It had all the markings of a perfectly staged and executed event. The weatherman was predicting drought for the next two weeks. Almost three hundred people came for the open house, and those who bought tickets were assured of good seats and good weather. A photographer was there from the Tyler *Morning News*. He took pictures of the wrestlers and of Claudius cutting the ribbon. They all were about to move inside and tour the facility when a car, blowing its horn and pulling an aluminum Airstream travel trailer, pulled off the main road and started toward them, whipping up so much dust behind it that it looked like it was dragging a tornado.

Someone in the crowd mentioned that the lieutenant governor of Texas had a trailer like that. The lieutenant governor was from Marshall, about fifty miles away, so it was possible. Sheriff Burl Jernigen stood under the billboard advertisement calling for his reelection, feeling proud. If it was the lieutenant governor, and if he could get his picture taken shaking hands with him in front of the billboard, shoot, he was as good as reelected.

The trouble was, the car pulling the trailer was an old Ford, and anybody who thought about it knew the lieutenant governor of Texas drove something fancier than a Ford. Even Squint knew that. Also, it and the trailer were covered with dead highway bugs, the kind you get from driving ninety miles an hour through the Louisiana swamps at night. There wasn't much windshield on the car to begin with, and what little there was was smeared with red dust and bug juice.

The car pulled up near the crowd and stopped. Two little eyeballs appeared in the only clear swipe of visibility that was available between dust and bugs. The eyes looked quickly at the crowd; then the door opened, and Louis Karp, a gnarled little man with long, thick sideburns and a hairline mustache, wearing a padded-shouldered, low-cut green suit and matching green cowboy boots, stepped out.

He didn't say a word. He just looked at the crowd with obvious contempt for a minute or two; then he went to work.

He opened the trunk of the car and took out a rusty log chain and two metal posts. Those he put down near the door to the trailer. Next, he unhooked two locking brackets on the sides of the trailer steps and pulled a catwalk straight out from under the trailer floor. The catwalk was six feet long and fitted into place so that the steps were on one end and the trailer door was on the other. He picked up the posts and fitted them in brackets on the catwalk about three feet from the door, through loops on the posts, and back to the other side of the door. With that done, he mounted the open end of the catwalk and stood with his hands on his hips, looking at the crowd.

Karp stomped his bootheel down twice on the catwalk as a signal, and the trailer began to roll around on its axle like a railroad boxcar on a bad track. The curtain in the door parted a space, and something looked out. Karp pointed at the door, which began creeping open. He couldn't get more attention from the crowd than he was getting. Sheriff Jernigen's hand moved involuntarily to the hogleg pistol on his hip.

The door suddenly banged open against the chains, and onto the catwalk stepped a man so big, strong, and ugly that every eye in the crowd widened and every mouth popped open, sucking for breath.

"Be careful," Karp said. "Don't make any sudden moves and get him excited, or those chains won't hold him for five seconds, and he's liable to come at you."

The monster stepped away from the trailer door. He wore a black velvet robe and high-topped black shoes. Wrestler's shoes. He came to the chain and gave the crowd a curious look, almost a bored look, the kind of look you get from a gorilla at the zoo. There was something about it that definitely wasn't human. Julie was hiding her face in the back of the Mask's neck; Sheriff Jernigen's hand was frozen above his gun; only Claudius, hands in pockets, his medal not even quivering a fraction on his chest, seemed unafraid.

"That's right," Karp went on, his voice no louder or softer than it needed to be, "stay calm now, and don't come any closer because I'm gonna have him turn around now and show you who he is."

Karp turned and made a circular motion with his finger. The monster seemed to understand and turned his back to the crowd. The white lettering on the back of the robe said "The Angel of Sorrow."

"Take off your robe," Karp said.

The Angel of Sorrow growled and showed his displeasure at being commanded by turning suddenly and swinging his monstrous arm at Karp's head.

"I said, 'Take off your robe.' " Karp's voice was crisp. In command.

The Angel, his back still turned toward the crowd, untied the robe and let it fall to the catwalk. Squint's first impression was that no man could be that hairy. Then he saw it wasn't hair that was running up the back of Angel's legs to his trunks and up from his trunks, under the arms and down to wide leather wristbands: It was feathers—long black feathers that looked like buzzard feathers. The Angel lifted his arms above his head and let his hands hang limply from the wrists, and the feathers, which were lying smooth, glued to elastic straps, suddenly stood up, unfurled at the movement.

"No man," Karp said, repeating it, "no man has ever been able to beat him. And not many men, no matter how strong they thought they were, have ever been strong enough to stay in the ring with him." He pointed at the Angel. "He's a killer, ladies and gentlemen, a killer with no conscience and no remorse. The woman who gave him birth, to this day, lives in a mental home in Baton Rouge. He snapped the spine of an alligator and ate him for dinner when he was only twelve years old. He's the Angel of Sorrow, ladies and gentlemen; he brings sorrow to the people's lives he visits, and he's visiting your lives because you've been bragging too much. . . ."

He pointed directly at Claudius Gains.

"*You've* been bragging too much," he said.

Claudius's eyes never moved, never blinked.

"You've been bragging too much, and we've heard you doing it, on radio, over in Houma, Louisiana, and that's why we've come among you.

"You're the one who did it," Karp went on, again pointing his finger at Claudius. "You wanted to fool these people in town into thinking the scurvy dogs you have here are wrestlers. Well, *there's* a wrestler." He pointed at the Angel of Sorrow. "And he's come here to take that ten thousand dollars off of you, not because he wants the money, but to teach you and all braggarts a lesson."

It was deadly still when Karp finished his speech. He looked at Claudius, for it was Claudius that he had called out for a response. Claudius gave him one. He turned to the Claw, choosing him from the four male wrestlers at his disposal. "Go over there and pop his tire," Claudius said.

Now the Claw wasn't a dummy. And he knew that Claudius was inviting trouble, but it seemed to him they were in trouble already, and he'd always done what Claudius asked. The crowd was so quiet you could hear them breathing as he walked over to the stout little tire the trailer rode on. He laid the sharp point of the claw in the groove between the tread and looked at Claudius, who nodded for him to go ahead.

There wasn't nothing else but to do it, and there was a small explosion, followed by a fast and steady hiss of air. The trailer began to sink to the rim of the tire as the catwalk began to thrust Karp and the Angel into the air. The crowd held its breath and waited.

It was like an artillery officer picking his target. Karp looked around, saw Brothers's motorcycle, and whispered instructions in the Angel's ear. Karp took down the chain, and the Angel stepped down from the catwalk. The crowd gave him plenty of room, a clear path between where he was and where he wanted to go, and he walked over to the motorcycle, turned it over on its side so that the sidecar was up in the air, bent down and sank his teeth into the sidecar wheel. The explosion was twice as loud as the trailer tire explosion and blew the Angel's head back. Despite the force of the explosion, the Angel of Sorrow was smiling.

24: The Aftermath

The afternoon passed. The photographers took pictures of everyone—Claudius, the wrestlers, Karp, and the Angel of Sorrow. There was a rush on the tickets, a second rush, as many of the people who were there saw the Angel, realized what a spectacle of blood and excitement was being offered them, and were suddenly anxious not to be left out. They bought extra tickets for their relatives, girl friends, and friends, not only for the first night of wrestling but for all three. Before the reporters and photographers rushed back to their offices to get out the next morning's paper, and before the crowd left to go home, Claudius sold over a thousand tickets. He waved good-bye to the last of them and locked the gates to the arena.

In the living room he handed the cashbox to Julie. She dumped the money from it onto the pool table, and Panzer and the Baron started helping her count it. In the kitchen Herman, Betty, and Rose worked on supper. They, like everybody else, had questions to ask of Claudius, but it was easy to see that Claudius was thinking, and so they held back. Claudius went to the refrigerator, took out a six-pack of beer, and carried it outside to his chair.

Squint, the Claw, Seymour, and the Mask were sitting in the shadow of the back porch. Claudius waved for them to follow him to the chair.

Suddenly there was a loud noise, a noise like metal being scraped, knocked, and ground against other metal. Claudius sat in the chair; the others stood looking toward the front of the house and arena from where the grinding noise was coming.

"Think of it this way," Claudius said. "If you're going to beat somebody, you've got to know what they're up to. You've got to study them and know what they're going to do *before* they do it." The Claw and Mask agreed.

Around the billboard wall and side of the house came the bug-splattered car pulling the trailer, the trailer riding on the rim of the flat tire, the back end dragging over the baked and crusted dirt. Karp ground to within thirty yards of the chair, and Claudius got up and waved for him to pull up.

"I said you could stay on my land, but that don't make you guests," Claudius yelled. Karp pulled up, but he obviously didn't hear Claudius because he got out of the car, smiled like he only wanted good things for everybody in the world, and waved.

"Did you ever in your life see a bigger weasel?" Claudius asked. "Look at him." When somebody wears a green plaid suit and green boots to match, there's not much choice but to look at him. "Reminds me of one of those South Texas loan sharks. Conscience thinner than the wings on a gnat."

Working without the help of the Angel—Claudius and the boys hadn't seen the Angel since he stood on the catwalk and posed for the photographers, growling and swinging at the popping flashbulbs, Karp finally having to back him into the trailer and lock the door from the outside—Karp went about the business of setting up the trailer. He cranked down the front leg and unhooked the car. He jacked up the flat and got the floor fairly level; then he pulled the catwalk out again and fixed it in place. Before he unlocked the trailer door and disappeared inside, he gave Claudius a last sweet wave.

"I want somebody in this chair at all times," Claudius said.

Squint took the first watch himself, kept company by old Seymour at the foot of the chair. He watched it get dark, saw the stars come out, and made his first wish.

"Never wish for something bad to happen." That was one of the rules Constance had told him. Another rule was: "Never wish for something greedy" because the sin of greed alone was enough to land you in the everlasting fire. The safest thing was to wish for something good for somebody else, and he and Julie used to make deals, each wishing something good for the other. The hardest rule of all was the one that said, "Thou art not allowed to tell thy wish to another living soul, or else it won't come true."

Now I can't tell you what Squint wished for because that would be against the rule. Squint wouldn't even tell Seymour, as Seymour was "living," and there was a better than even chance that he did have a soul. I can and will tell you, however, that the wish was a good one, wasn't too selfish or greedy, and did, in fact, come true. This story began, if you remember, on a bad note with a funeral; the first part ends here with Squint's wish, on a good note.

PART TWO

25: Putting the Feet to Work

Those who haven't tried a summer in East Texas really ought to give it a try. Summer really begins in spring with warm days and cool nights and hurricanes on the Gulf Coast. That means a week or more of rain for the folks in Tyler. Then comes the first hot spell, days in the low 90s and nights in the low 80s, usually ending with more rain. Early summer comes on then, and the thermometer flirts around the 100-degree mark. Nobody has to go out of his way to get a suntan, but the people in Texas don't exactly love the sun the way people in California and Florida love it. They look forward to its going down at night and giving them a small measure of relief. On a "cool" night, the temperature drops to something like 88 degrees or, on a good night, 85 degrees. And that's only June. After June comes the real summer.

Squint tossed and rolled all night in the heat. He'd been replaced in the chair by Panzer, and Panzer, eventually, by Claudius. Sometime after midnight Squint got out of bed and looked out the window to the side yard. From his bedroom he could see a light burning in the window of the trailer, a small light, not much brighter than the moon. He could also see Claudius, not sitting in the chair but pacing around it, talking to himself, every so often kicking a clod of dirt like he was in deep thought or deep trouble. Finally, with no breeze through his bedroom at all, Squint went to sleep.

It was already midmorning when he opened his eyes. If he'd slept five more minutes, Herman would have come upstairs and checked him for signs of life. All the cars and trucks, including Karp's, were gone, and the thinking chair outside was empty. Karp had left early, before seven, dressed again in his green suit and boots, and Claudius had jumped in a car and followed him. Everybody except Herman and Squint, who they decided to let sleep late, was in town hoofing it from door to door, selling tickets. Seymour had gone with them.

Later in the afternoon they came staggering back: Betty and Rose, Panzer and the Baron from working the downtown, the Mask and Julie from working the grocery stores, the Claw and Brothers and Seymour, who'd gotten the housewives at home. Herman had a kettle of stew waiting on the stove for them and fed them in waves. Twice housewives had telephoned the police, hysterical about a man with a claw, a bear, and another man drinking whiskey on their front porches. Everybody was tired and footsore, but they'd sold another three hundred tickets, including a bunch to the squad of police who came to arrest them and to the women who'd called the police.

Karp came back, then Claudius, in as foul a mood as anyone had ever seen him. He had under his arm the afternoon newspaper, which he opened to the sports page and tossed in the middle of the table. "I want a beer and something to eat," he said, sitting at the corner of the table and kicking off his shoes. His shoulders were slumped from the heat and humidity; his ankles, when he rolled down his socks, reminded Squint of Saturday morning when all the kids got to go to the city pool. The lifeguard would keep rolling up dirt on their ankles with his thumb, and sometimes he'd send them back to the shower room four or five times. "And bring me some hot water," Claudius said.

Herman brought all three, the beer, wisely, first. Squint and everybody else looked at the paper.

The undisputed highlight of the page was a large picture of the Angel of Sorrow rattling his chains with his left hand and reaching for the photographer's face with his right. There were other pictures on the page, of the ring and of the wrestlers standing around it, but the picture that was second most in importance was one of Claudius, looking for all the world like somebody had just poured hog slop down the back of his pants. Under his picture it said, "Gains gives anguished look for photographers."

The water in the pan steamed around his rolled cuffs as Claudius rubbed one foot with the other and finished his bowl of stew. "Read the third paragraph," he said, and Squint started reading.

"According to the manager, Louis Karp, the Angel has been barred from wrestling in nine states, including Mississippi, Tennessee, Kentucky, Illinois, Indiana, and Ohio—"

"Not that part, the last part," Claudius told him.

Squint skipped down.

" 'The Angel wants to be fair,' Karp said. 'He's willing to wrestle all four of them at the same time, but he'll do it the right way. The first night he'll take on the two old fat ones; the second night he'll tear apart the two goofy little pups; the third night he'll take on all four or anybody who can walk.' "

"That's the part," Claudius said.

Now all the wrestlers were mad. "Old fat ones," the Baron said. They were standing shoulder to shoulder around the table, and the Claw stuck his hook out in the middle.

"I'm going to stick this up his nose and twist it," he said. Then he smiled, but not what you'd call a very friendly smile.

"You get one leg, and I'll get the other one," the Baron said, making a motion to Panzer that was like breaking a big pulley bone. "We'll see what his innards look like."

Claudius took his feet out of the water and dried them. "You're gonna do nothing of the sort," he said, and for a minute the Claw and the Baron thought Claudius had gone soft. He got up from the chair and smiled and said, "We're all going to be as nice as we can be." Then he poured the nasty black pan of foot water in the stew and said, "Somebody take this out to them and see if they're hungry." That was the Claudius they knew; that was the Claudius that would guide them through this time of crisis.

26: Getting Ready

Herman had nine heads of cabbage stacked on the kitchen counter like cannonballs. Squint was looking for something to do to help as everyone worked to get ready for the first exhibition, scheduled to begin in eight hours. Herman was making coleslaw for the hot dogs they planned to sell. Three hundred hot dogs they had figured for two thousand people. The meat cleaver moved like a greased machine in Herman's hand, his fingers on the other hand darting in and out of danger in rhythm to the whop whop-whop-whop-scrape, whop-whop-whop-scrape.

Squint was smart enough not to say anything while Herman was chopping. "Anything I can do to help?" he asked as Herman finished one head and reached for another.

"Make some room in the refrigerator," Herman said. He had two five-gallon jars to fill and get in there.

To make room, Squint had only to move two shelves of Claudius's beer to make one shelf. It was about the coolest job he could have, considering the temperature outside, so he took his time and stacked them tight. All the cans fitted except one, and it occurred to Squint that he'd never tasted beer.

Betty and Rose were working in a concession area

to the left of the front porch steps. The Baron and Panzer had planted some fence posts in the ground in front of the porch and hammered together a make-shift counter. Betty and Rose were loading a rented Coke cooler with ice and bottles of pop. "Look at the big shot," Betty said, seeing Squint with the open can of beer in his hand.

It didn't taste exactly like he thought it would. It was bitter, like vinegar water or the sulfur water his mother had once made him drink to cure the worms. He hadn't had worms, only she thought he had because one of the kids at school had them, and he'd pretended to be sick so he could slip away and do some fishing. The beer tasted worse because it bubbled, gave him the hiccups, and made him belch.

"I'll trade you this for an RC," he offered, but Rose wouldn't hear of it.

"Oh, no," she said, "you opened it; you drink it."

He tried to find Seymour, but Seymour had crawled under the house to get out of the sun, and nothing could coax him out. "Beer for you, Seymour," Squint whispered. "Beer for the bear." The bear loved beer, only he hated hot weather more.

Now one beer won't make a feller drunk, but on a hot day and when you're only eleven years old and it's your first ever, it will make you dizzy. After he was half done with it, it didn't taste so bad anymore; in fact, it tasted good. It made him feel light-headed and pleasant, and he could easily understand why people drank it and why his mother considered it one of the vilest activities that man could take part in. That her own husband drank beer, and that she couldn't do anything about it, must have been a constant embarrassment between her and her church friends. He wondered whether or not she'd ever tasted beer and decided probably not.

She wouldn't have liked anything that was happening, not the wrestling arena in the front yard (Wrestling! People hurting each other for profit! Ugliness and fun while people could be doing the Lord's work!). Not all the new and crazy people living in her house, and certainly not him drinking a whole can, not even the *thought* of him drinking a whole can. He didn't feel good about it and had decided for himself not to drink any more, ever, unless he was trapped in the desert somewhere and it was a matter of life and death. He was, after all, a reasonable person.

Panzer and the Baron were in their trunks and practicing in the ring. Claudius, the Mask, and Julie were in town on a trip to pick up more stuff for the opening. The Claw was in the thinking chair, keeping an eye on the trailer. Squint walked down to the bleachers beside the ring and watched Panzer and the Baron make their plans.

There had been a movie come to town earlier that year, one where this spaceship came and landed in Washington, D.C.; on board the spaceship were a regular man and a big, invincible robot who could melt iron with a ray beam from his helmet. The whole world was threatened, so they had to stop making war on each other at once and start living in peace, or else this big robot, who was a kind of space policeman, would come back and destroy them all.

That was what was happening now, Squint decided. Everybody at the farm was being threatened by the Angel of Sorrow, and whatever else they did, they had to stick together. Everybody had to trust each other to do the right thing.

Panzer, in the ring, suddenly had an idea. He walked around the ropes, examining the padded steel posts in the corners, testing the padding. "Run up to the house and bring me a knife," Panzer told Squint, and in a few minutes Squint was back with one. Panzer pulled the padding away from the pole that would be in their corner, cut open the back, and started ripping out the cotton padding. When he was finished, you couldn't tell it was gone.

"Here's what we do," he said. "We get him in trouble, any kind of trouble, then you grab one arm and I grab his other. . . ." Panzer got the Baron in position, and they pantomimed holding the Angel each by an invisible arm. "Then we take him headfirst into the post." They ran at the post and stopped short of hurting themselves.

The Baron tested the hardness with his hand. "Yeah," he said. "Bust his head open."

Squint, seeing it all, had to grimace. The cooperation was admirable, just like in the movie. The only problem was with the tactics, which were, first of all, dishonest and, second of all, unrealistic. What was the Angel going to do, hold out his arms?

"Yeah," the Baron said. They shook hands.

"Yeah," Panzer said back.

There were only three hours left to go before the opening of the gates when Claudius, Julie, and the Mask came back from town. Both the Mask and Claudius had cardboard boxes in their arms. The Mask took his upstairs, and Claudius took his to the kitchen, to the refrigerator to pick up a couple of beers, then back to the hall.

"Somebody who ain't doing anything, come downstairs," he yelled. He didn't have to yell because Squint was right behind him. Panzer and the Baron, Betty and Rose, everybody who was going to have to wrestle that night was upstairs in bed resting. Everybody else had something to do except Squint, and of course, he was right behind Claudius. Squint had been looking for something to do all day.

The task his father had for him wasn't much. He cut old newspapers into strips the width and length of five-dollar bills, while Claudius put real five-dollar bills face up and bottom side down around the stacks of newspaper. The cutting and stacking gave them time to talk for the first time, it seemed, in days.

"How come you squint your eyes like you do?" Claudius asked.

"I wasn't aware that I was," Squint said, concentrating on his scissors. "People tell me I do it, but I can never tell."

"First chance we get, I'm gonna take you down and have your eyes tested. Maybe it's because you need glasses."

"They already been tested by everybody, and everybody says it's a bad habit." There were more important things to talk about than his squinting—the wrestling, for instance—and he asked Claudius what was going to happen.

Claudius looked at his son and felt inadequate. "All of this might not work out," he said. "Everything we're doing may turn out bad. We may not get enough people, and the bank may run us off the place. The Angel of Sorrow . . . I did some telephoning today and found out some things."

Squint didn't look up from his work.

"I found out among other things that he's a renegade. I found out he's crazy, or Karp's crazy. They've been making trouble for everybody in the wrestling business for years, and I don't know if it's true or not, but up in Kansas a few years back, he broke a fellow's neck."

That made Squint look up.

"Broke it clean. Some say it was an accident, and some say he done it on purpose. Don't matter to the guy with the broken neck. Karp collected some big prize money and bought that trailer they ride around in."

Claudius began the next phase of the operation, binding the bills and strips of newspaper with official money wrappers from the bank and packing them snugly in a briefcase.

"So what are we going to do?" Squint finally asked.

"We're just gonna have to find some way to beat him. We've got an arena out there, and the people will come these first three nights, and we ought to get enough to pay off the bank. But after it's over, we're back in the same place if we don't win. Ain't nobody gonna come see a bunch of clowns."

The last stack Claudius put in the briefcase was a stack of real fives. "Go upstairs and get the Claw," he asked Squint.

Squint came back with the Claw, and Claudius closed the case and, with a pair of handcuffs borrowed from the sheriff, cuffed it to the Claw's good hand.

"It's one of the oldest tricks in the world," Claudius admitted, "but if nobody gets too close to it, it ought to work."

"What happens if we lose and we have to give it to them?" Squint asked.

Claudius shook his head in pain. It was his misfortune to go through life explaining things to people. "First of all, we're not going to lose. Second of all, we can't afford to lose. And third of all, even if we do, we can always think of something."

The Claw felt awkward with the hook on one arm and the briefcase on the other and looked to Claudius for help.

"How's this?" Claudius said. "If we lose, we cut off your good hand and say the money was stolen." Squint and the Claw thought that was awful. "Can't anybody around here take a joke?" Claudius said.

Nobody wanted to admit it, but they all were a bit nervous.

They had spent the whole day, it seemed like forever, getting ready, and finally, they were. All that was left to do was to set up the front porch for Durwood Henry's broadcasting, and this they did by bringing out a table and a chair and running an extension cord from the living room.

When the Navy launches a new ship, they get a pretty girl to break a bottle of champagne on the bow. Claudius didn't have any champagne, and he wasn't about to waste any of his beer on a mere ritual, but he thought something ought to be done, so he took Constance's picture and hung it on the main gate so everyone could see it on the way in. Underneath it, he taped up a card that said "In Memoriam." The picture hung between two of his wrestling posters.

Durwood Henry came and set up the table. He plugged in his portable broadcasting equipment and let it start warming up. On the table he put out his signs, THE DURWOOD HENRY SHOW and KRIT. Next to his table was another one, one with FIRST AID draping down the front.

The concession stand was ready, and a banner had been hung between the two porch posts behind it: HOT DOGS 25¢ SOFT DRINKS 15¢.

The Panzer, the Baron, Betty and Rose were all dressed for their bouts.

Claudius was wearing his frock coat and his Stetson, and he had his medal on his chest. The Mask rolled a stand-up microphone to the middle of the porch and adjusted it to Claudius's height. Claudius turned the mike on and started tapping with his finger.

Squint stood on the top row of the bleachers near the front gate. A photographer came out of the house and said something to Claudius that the microphone didn't pick up. Then he started setting up his camera on a tripod in front of the porch.

"Testing, one, two, three. Can you hear me up there?"

Squint could hear him fine and waved his arm.

"Okay," Claudius announced. "Everybody who wants to get their picture taken come on out here so we can get it over with."

It was a picture never to be duplicated. Julie came out wearing a white nurse's uniform and sat down at the first-aid table. Claudius and Squint stood beside the microphone; Durwood sat at the broadcast table. Betty and Rose came out, followed by Panzer and the Baron, all wearing their wrestling outfits. The Mask sat on the edge of the porch, holding a chain that led down to Seymour, wearing his red and white checkered wrestling trunks. The Claw stood on the steps, the briefcase open to show off the money inside. Next to him stood Sheriff Jernigen, his badge hanging from the pocket of a black and white striped referee's shirt, his.

Herman, wearing an apron, stood ready behind the makeshift counter of the concession stand.

The first flashbulb went off, and then another, and then a third. When their eyes cleared and they could see again, they noticed that Karp and the Angel had come into the arena and were standing with their backs to the ring, watching them.

"Very pretty," Karp said; his tone was sarcastic and his face was full of everything but love. He looked like the weasel Claudius had accused him of being. The Claw snapped the briefcase closed and stepped behind the sheriff. Claudius came down to see what they wanted.

"As I said before," Karp said, "it ain't the money I'm interested in, but I'm glad I saw it."

"You saw it," Claudius said.

"Now that I saw it"—Karp smiled—"I want it, and if I don't get it when all this is over, and if it ain't all there, ten thousand dollars to the penny, the Angel is going to slowly and painfully chew your face off."

Karp and the Angel left then, and Claudius came back to the porch.

"I say we don't waste any time," Panzer said. "I say we bust his head first thing."

Claudius looked at the sheriff and said, "Let me hear you count to three."

"One . . . two . . . three," the sheriff said, his voice keeping a regular cadence.

"Too slow," Claudius said. "Faster."

"Onetwothree."

Claudius nodded his head. "Good. That's it. If they

get that animal down, even for a hot second, that's the way you count."

They were at last ready. A crowd of people was standing at the gate, admiring the picture of Constance Gains, and Claudius put on his Stetson, took his roll of tickets and money box, and started toward the gate.

27: It Begins

Claudius had hoped for eighteen hundred people, but he hadn't expected them; what he'd expected was more like a thousand and three or four hundred, and what he'd been willing to settle for was a thousand even. They came in greater numbers than anyone in his right mind would have ever dreamed. They came four, five, and six to a car; they came in farm trucks; one man brought his aged parents in an ambulance; two or three people came to the bouts by taxi; a nearby farmer came over the fields on his tractor, his wife riding on the fender beside him. Some had seen Claudius's wrestlers in the ring in Dallas; more than a few had big, strong, fun-loving hods for sons and were considering enrolling them in the wrestling academy. A few people, women mostly, loved wrestling so much they'd insisted on kissing Claudius's hands for bringing it all into Tyler. The biggest reason they all came, however, was to see and watch the Angel of Sorrow. In their minds the Angel was probably meaner, and uglier, than the devil himself.

One of the cars had six people in it, a weather-beaten man of fifty-some-odd years and his wife, his grown son and his son's wife, and their son, Bubba, dressed in a fringed cowboy outfit complete with hat, cap pistol, and lariat. There was also a heavyset un-married daughter, in whose lap Bubba sat.

The poor Claw had been pressed into service again, this time to direct the traffic in the field in front of the arena. Claudius had stuck a cardboard sign, PARKING, to the side of the briefcase, and the Claw was waving it, trying to get people to park in some kind of orderly fashion.

"Bubba, look at that poor man," the grandmother said. "He's only got one hand." Bubba pulled his cap gun and pretended to shoot the Claw; then he got a better idea. His lasso had been waiting for the right target all day, and there it was, waving in the twilight in front of him.

One second the Claw was standing there, doing his job; the next second there was a rope around his hook, and he was almost jerked off his feet. He had to run like a madman to keep from getting dragged by the car. Bubba had looped the rope around the doorknob of the car and was laughing his seven-year-old guts out.

The unmarried daughter tried to untangle the rope, but couldn't; it wasn't tangled, but tied. The old man driving hadn't heard a clear word through his ears since he was fifty and had no idea what the shouting outside the car was about. The only reason he stopped was that he found a good place to park, way in the back behind the other cars, where nobody would hit him. Immediately the back door flew open, and Bubba took off in a run, his mother, father, and unmarried aunt after him.

Now the average wrestling fan believes in working hard when it's time to work and playing hard when it's time to play. The thing he never forgets or forgives is somebody trying to cheat him out of either one, working or playing. It is all right for wrestlers to cheat each other; a wrestling fan is usually *for* cheating, so long as the one who cheats gets what he deserves in the end. It's also permitted to cheat back, once somebody cheats you. Claudius would have been a poor promoter of wrestling if he hadn't understood that. That's why he planned so many show business touches, to make sure the crowd didn't feel cheated. That's also why he couldn't do any really bad cheating until the third night.

With five minutes left to go before time to start, Claudius sold the last six tickets, to the little cowboy, Bubba, and his family.

"Ordinarily I like kids," the Claw said, coming from the parking lot to relieve Claudius at the gate and sell either standing room for a dollar or tickets to the next night's matches to stragglers who came late. Bubba was in, and it was too late to keep him out; his mother had foolishly allowed him to keep the rope. "That's one kid I'd like to have for five minutes, though," the Claw said. "Just five minutes."

Claudius went to the porch to get things going.

Upstairs in his bedroom, Squint put on the khaki shirt and pants Claudius had brought him from town and strung the dark green necktie around the collar and tied it. Then he put on the cap and looked at himself in the mirror. He looked ridiculous. The whole idea was ridiculous, him wearing such an outfit, and there wasn't anybody in the world who could've got him to do it except Claudius.

In the aisle around the arena, Seymour and the Mask were entertaining the crowd. Seymour would lay his head in some fat woman's lap, and the woman would just about have a baby laughing.

Bubba took one look at that bear and started getting his lasso ready. Seymour took one look at Bubba and called it quits, pulling the Mask behind him to the safety of the front porch. Seymour was an old bear, and the way he'd gotten to be an old bear was by recognizing trouble when he saw it and getting out of its way.

"Ladies and gentlemen, give me your attention please." The arena was filled with Claudius's voice. He stood in the middle of the porch with his hands on the microphone. "I want to welcome you to the Constance M. Gains Memorial Arena. . . ." Behind him on the porch, the Baron and Panzer held open the screen door and rolled the jukebox outside. Behind them came Squint, dressed in the makeshift army uniform, carrying the borrowed American flag. "Tonight we pay tribute to the United States Army and all the brave men who served our country in war." There were cheers in the arena. "Please stand for the playing of the national anthem."

Claudius lowered the mike on its stand, placed it in front of the jukebox, and punched A-1 on the selector buttons. The mechanical arm groaned and brought down the record, and the United States Marine Band began playing a scratchy version of "The Star-Spangled Banner."

Men stood in the bleachers, their hands held over their hearts. The Claw stood at the gate. He couldn't hold his right hand over his heart because the briefcase was locked to it, so he placed his hook over his heart instead. Claudius and the Mask on the porch had their hands over their hearts, and Seymour, obviously moved by the solemnity of the occasion, tried to do likewise. In the dying strains of "and the home . . . of the . . . brave" the bear lost his balance and fell back to all fours, and that jarred the porch, and that made the needle on the record skip back to "and the rockets' red glare, the bombs bursting in air." There wasn't nothing to do but let it play on through the second time.

28: Badlands Betty and Rose La Rue

Squint put the flag in the staff on the porch post, his duties temporarily at an end. In the front room Betty and Rose were ready to go down to the ring, waiting only for their introductions. Claudius began announcing again as Squint climbed the steps to his room.

Claudius first introduced a man who needed no introduction, except that some people might not recognize him the way he was dressed, a man who had been keeping the peace in Tyler for longer than most folks could remember, a man noted for his sense of justice and fair play, Tyler's own Sheriff Burl Jernigen.

Squint watched the crowd from the bedroom window and judged their clapping and hooting to be a little more approving than disapproving. One person re-marked how good the sheriff looked in stripes.

And for the folks who weren't fortunate enough to be there in person, Claudius introduced Durwood Henry, who'd be broadcasting the matches from the sports desk on the porch. Squint turned on the table radio in his room and started getting undressed.

The radio came on station with another of KRIT's famous commercials.

". . . so if you haven't thought about it before, think about it now. Minks thrive in this climate, they eat practically nothing, and reproduce, well, I don't have to tell you how minks reproduce, but they love having those babies. We'll get you started in mink ranching; just write MINK, that's M-I-N-K, in care of radio station KRIT, Tyler, Texas."

Betty and Rose climbed into the ring. Squint threw the army uniform back in the box Claudius brought from town and started putting on his regular clothes.

"We're back," Durwood told the radio audience, "and in the preliminary match, we have Badlands Betty Brown against Rosemary La Rue, the Rose of Texas, who Badlands Betty calls the Yellow Rose of Texas, but everybody who's seen Rose wrestle knows she's anything but yellow."

Durwood went on to describe their outfits and how

they came to get them. Badlands Betty was wearing the skin of a renegade leopard that had broken out of a traveling circus and terrorized the countryside for months before it made the mistake of going after Betty's little dog, Scotty. Rosemary La Rue was wearing the mark of royalty, a high-topped silver perfumed wig, passed down in her family all the way from the court of King Louie the Fourteenth.

"The preliminary will be three falls, with a ten-minute time limit for each fall. It promises to be exciting," Durwood went on. "But most of the folks here are waiting to see the main event, the first of the challenge matches between the Baron and Panzer Kaufman on one team, and the Angel of Sorrow on the other, the Angel who goes by the name of Sorrow, who might indeed be the world's meanest man . . ."

The bell rang to start the match. After a few minutes of watching Betty and Rose's exhibition, Squint turned to the side window, to the trailer outside and the Angel of Sorrow.

The Angel was standing, silhouetted in the doorway, filling the doorway almost, his shoulders and arms wider than the light. As Squint watched, the Angel moved out of the way, and Karp, by contrast a midget, stepped through. Karp closed the door behind him and started toward the house.

There was nobody in the house to stop him, Squint

realized, and took off downstairs to the kitchen.

"It's starting to get rough," Durwood Henry was reporting. "Badlands Betty has the Rose on the mat and has her knee on her throat."

Squint was there to keep Karp from just walking through the house. Karp stepped into the kitchen, but he stopped at the door when he saw Squint. He had an unlit match in his mouth and flipped it from one side to the other. "Go get your daddy," he said, "and tell him I want to talk."

Squint found Claudius at ringside, keeping time on the falls, and gave him the message. Claudius looked at his watch and rang the bell for the first fall to end, then called the Mask over to take his place.

When they got to the kitchen, Karp wasn't there. Nor was he on the back porch, in the hall, or in the bathroom. He wouldn't have gone upstairs because all that was up there was bedrooms. It suddenly occurred to Claudius that Karp had gone downstairs, to the cellar. Squint was a half second ahead of him, already moving to the cellar door.

Karp was there, all right, smiling, waving hello in suspicious friendship. "I thought this might be a good quiet place," he said. Karp stood near the table where the "money" had been cut, picked up the scissors that were still there, and started cleaning his fingernails. Upstairs in the arena there was a loud outburst of cheering. Claudius and Squint came down and quickly looked around the room. On top of one of Constance's former end tables and in full sight of everyone were the leftover money wrappers from the bank.

"Nice crowd you got up there tonight," Karp said. Squint calmly turned and even more calmly climbed the steps again for the hall and kitchen. Claudius was puzzled but let him go.

"It's a good crowd," Claudius said, circling the little man so as to draw his attention away from the money wrappers. "Say what you want to say."

Karp held up five fingers and sat on the couch. "Five seconds, the Angel can finish your boys off in five seconds if I tell him to. I know it, you know it, and they know it, but the Angel ain't gonna do that."

"You come to offer me a deal?"

Squint came back to the cellar again, this time bringing with him a tray and two cans of beer. He put the tray on the end table and covered the wrappers.

"You're a good showman; I can tell because I'm a good showman myself. How'd you like to work for me?" Karp asked Claudius. "I mean, when all this is over."

If Claudius was angry, he didn't show it. "Karp, I'm gonna tell you something. I know twice as much about show business as you'll ever know, and I'll tell you something else: I don't know whether you know it or not, but you're *already* working for me."

Karp held up his five fingers again. "Like I say, five seconds. I tell the Angel to get 'em, and them two peckerwoods are done. If I say, 'Angel, *hurt 'em,*' they're gonna be needing wheelchairs and Seeing Eye dogs, but I ain't gonna say it 'cause it would be bad for business."

Karp finished his can of beer. "So here's what I came to tell you. The Angel is going to carry your boys the first two falls. Nothing gets serious, and nobody gets hurt until the third fall. . . . Is it a deal?"

The advantages of the deal were painfully more attractive than the disadvantages. Claudius gave Karp's offer a moment's thought, then accepted it.

Karp had gotten up from the couch and was looking at one of the support beams that held up the house. "Nice house," he said. "They don't make them like this anymore." As he started up the stairs to leave, the bell outside clanged, and the second fall came to an end. They listened to the crowd cheering again, and Karp smiled. "Karp's Arena. Got a nice sound to it, don't it?"

Squint followed him out and watched him go in the trailer.

The third fall between Betty and Rose was under way when Squint came back to the porch. Betty had her claws out like a panther and was stalking Rose around the ring, taking slashes at her face with her fingernails. Rose let herself get trapped in a corner; Betty went for the head at the same time Rose went for the body. In a moment, Betty had Rose in a head-lock, and when Rose broke it, there was a trickle of blood on Rose's cheek. The sheriff stopped the match to look at the "wound" and called Julie to come from the first-aid table. The crowd applauded for Julie in her cute nurse's uniform as she wiped Rose's cheek with a piece of gauze and covered the scratch with a Band-Aid. Time was running out in the fall, and in the remaining minutes the two women wrestled to a standoff. When the final bell rang, the sheriff raised both women's arms in victory, and Claudius announced the draw.

Rose put her robe on and looked for the tall silver wig she'd left on the post in her corner. A little kid in a cowboy suit was wearing it in the aisle by the ring, and she had to chase the kid into Betty's arms on the other side to get it back.

"There's gonna be a fifteen-minute intermission, folks," Claudius announced. He invited them all to try the hot dogs and cold drinks at the concession stand. "You'd better stock up because the next match is gonna be a killer."

29: The Baron and Panzer Show Their Stuff

The intermission took more like thirty minutes than fifteen because of the rush on the concession stand. Claudius, Squint, the Mask, and Julie all helped out, Claudius doing more socializing and glad-handing with old friends than selling hot dogs. Tyler was a small place, and just about everybody knew everybody else. The intermission was just about as noisy as the first match.

When it was over, Claudius took a few minutes to talk to his wrestlers. "The Angel's the challenger," he told them, "which means he enters the ring first. We let him wait on us, so maybe he'll get a little nervous."

Panzer and the Baron didn't admit it, but they'd as soon the intermission lasted for hours; if they had their way, the Angel would wait forever. Or even longer. They were leaning forward against the pool table while Betty and Rose, now dressed once again in street clothes, massaged their arms and backs.

The noise coming from the arena outside was suddenly gone. An overpowering hush fell over everything, sweeping like a wave from the front of the arena into the room where they stood. It was as if everything was afraid to move, even the air. "Now what we've got to do is . . ." Claudius was saying; then he too was taken by the silence. He turned quickly to the screen door to see what was happening.

The Angel of Sorrow had entered the arena. He'd come in through the main gate and had walked almost unnoticed to the side of the ring, taken off his robe, and flexed the black feathers along his back and legs. He stood like a frozen Goliath, his hands on his hips in a warlike pose as the words and breaths of the crowd sucked back in. If one person had panicked, they all might have panicked; it was lucky that no one moved.

The first sounds that came filtering back were the sounds of Durwood Henry whispering into the microphone. "There's nothing wrong with your sets, ladies and gentlemen. The reason it's so quiet is because the Angel of Sorrow, just like he popped through a trap-door, all of a sudden is standing at ringside. I'm telling you, this crowd is getting something it didn't expect, and I'm not sure they like it. Right now they're thinking they'd rather be where you are, safe at home listening on radio."

"Come on," Claudius said, "we'd better get out there."

Which was exactly what they had to do. When they saw Panzer and the Baron on the front porch, there was a wave of instant relief as the crowd remembered what it was there for, to sit back out of danger in the stands and watch somebody else take the chances.

"Listen, boys"—Claudius gave last-minute instructions—"I've made a deal with Karp, and nobody gets hurt until the third fall. He's not expecting anything till then, so if you get a chance to get him, take it. It may be the only chance you've got."

"We'll get him," the Baron said, but his mouth was saying one thing and his eyes were saying another.

"Folks," Durwood said, "there's no way I can tell you what a brave thing Panzer Kaufman and the Baron are doing. It's two against one, I know, and the Baron and Panzer are no punies. But they're getting kind of old, and getting in the ring with that monster is like getting in with Frankenstein."

Claudius walked to the side of the ring with them, talking all the way. "Take it slow; feel him out. We don't know; he may be slow. We don't know, but maybe he can't see out of his left eye. Fake him out on the soft posts first; then let him have it full speed. And don't worry about killing him 'cause if anything could kill him, he'd be dead by now." They arrived at the ring, and Claudius wished them luck. "Remember, you're doing this for all of us . . . for their future" —he pointed at Squint and Julie on the front porch— "and for your own retirement, and haven't you always wanted a home of your own? Well, this is your chance to get it."

That was all the encouragement they needed. The

sheriff motioned them into the ring, and Claudius went back to the PA system on the porch to make the announcement.

Squint decided to watch from the roof, for a purpose, so back up to his bedroom he went and out the window. Before the arena had gone up, he could sit with his back against the house between his and Julie's windows and smoke an occasional cigarette or watch the road for hours. It used to be nobody could see him, but that was changed now. Now it was one of the best seats in the arena, but not really part of the arena. He figured he could watch what was going to happen and not have a real part in it. There wasn't anything he or anybody could do to help the Baron or Panzer, but if he could see something nobody else saw, some way to beat the Angel, then that would be the most important thing. He put the portable radio in the window so he could hear what Durwood Henry was saying.

The bell rang to start the first fall.

"It's not really two against one yet," Durwood announced. "Following the rules of tag-team wrestling, the Baron is waiting outside the ropes in the corner while Panzer Kaufman takes on the big fellow first. Remember, Panzer has to make skin contact with the Baron before the Baron can take his place in the ring."

Panzer and the Angel came together in the center

of the ring and joined in the traditional starting position, leaning in toward each other with their heads
touching and their arms on each other's shoulders.
From that position, neither wrestler had the advantage
over the other, and like in Steal the Bacon, the one with
the quickest reflexes would get the first hold.

It was the Angel who made the first move. He
jumped backward, away from Panzer's grip, then
spread his arms and moved back in to grab Panzer in
a bear hug. It didn't work because Panzer, a foot and
a half shorter and at least 150 pounds lighter on his
feet, ducked under the arms and moved closer to the
Baron in the corner. The Angel, still determined to
get the bear hug, came after him and made a second,
even slower and more awkward grab. Panzer again
ducked out of the way, but this time he stepped up
behind the Angel and swung the back of his elbow
into the back of the Angel's head. The Angel made the
mistake of stepping even closer to the Baron, and the
Baron leaned over the top rope and smashed his meaty
forearm into the Angel's face.

Whether Squint wanted to get involved or not, he
was involved, and he moved to the edge of the porch
to let his legs hang over. Standing directly below him
was Claudius, who had jerked the white Stetson from
his head and was nervously fingering the brim. "Oh,
sweet Jesus," Claudius said, rolling his eyes up to

Squint but not really seeing him. "It didn't even hurt him."

Technically the Baron's whopping the Angel in the face from outside the ring was cheating, and the sheriff shook his finger in the Baron's direction as a warning. Panzer and the Angel went back to the starting position, and this time Panzer took the initiative, getting the Angel in a half nelson and tripping him face forward to the mat. Panzer had the advantage then and kept it, releasing the Angel's arm and springing high to land in the middle of the Angel's back. The Angel seemed to offer no resistance as Panzer locked his legs around the Angel's middle and started pulling his massive head backward by the chin.

"If there's anybody out there who thinks wrestling is a fake, I can only say I wish they were here to see what's going on in this ring tonight. Panzer Kaufman has the Angel of Sorrow in a chin hold and is trying, really trying, to tear his head off. And wait . . . the Angel, in spite of the pain he must be in, is getting to his feet."

Durwood Henry was calling it right. The Angel was getting his knees and arms under him, and Panzer was about to play horsey like some little kid on his daddy's back.

Then the Angel was on his feet, and Panzer was riding piggyback. He still had the chin hold, so the Angel couldn't see where he was staggering. Again he staggered toward the Baron's corner, and again the Baron leaned over the ropes to deliver a forearm, only this time, just as the Baron launched the blow, Karp yelled, "Duck!" and the forearm sailed over the Angel's head and knocked Panzer senseless.

Ordinarily that would have been the end of hostilities; Panzer was helpless, and the Angel could get an easy pin. But these were special circumstances, and the sheriff ruled that Panzer and the Baron had indeed made physical contact, and the Baron was allowed to climb in the ring and carry on for the groggy Panzer. Panzer managed to crawl to safety, and the Baron wrestled safely, wisely staying out of the Angel's way till the end of the first fall.

Despite the evidence that pointed against it and probably to give them hope, Claudius gathered the Baron and Panzer back to the living room and told them what a good job they were doing. He set up two shot glasses on the bar and poured them brim full with raw whiskey from Brothers's bottle, and when the wrestlers tried to lift them, it was hard to tell whose hand was shaking worse.

"Yeah," the Baron muttered. "We got him right where we want him."

Panzer emptied the whiskey into his throat and grabbed the bottle from Claudius's hand. He and the

Baron shared guzzles till Claudius took the bottle back.

"Easy on that stuff." He looked at his watch and groaned. "Three minutes to think of something."

Back in the ring, the Angel of Sorrow sat on a stool in his corner like a boxer while Karp dipped a sponge in a bucket of water and squeezed it over his head and shoulders. The Masked Marvel and Seymour came walking by below them, and Seymour made the mistake of stopping to sniff the Angel's shoe. The Angel gave a flick with his foot and kicked the bear in the nose. The crowd made its displeasure known, and Karp walked around the ring, shaking his fist at them. The noble Seymour jerked his chain from the Mask's hand, forced his way between two women on the front row, and crawled beneath the bleachers.

Claudius thought of something that might work. Panzer and the Baron held their noses from the stink of some kind of milky fluid that Claudius was spraying under their arms. "Don't act like babies, and hold still," he told them. "It ain't nothing but roach killer."

Claudius thought that if they could get the Angel in a headlock, the bug spray would sting him in the eyes. It wasn't much of a plan, but it was all he could think of.

The bell called them back to the ring, this time for

the Baron to start and Panzer to wait for the tag. The
Baron and the Angel met in the middle, the Claw rang
the bell, and time started on the second fall. The wrestling that followed was more funny than serious, but
the fans loved it just the same.

According to the rules of exhibition wrestling, a
combatant may not choke, pull hair, gouge eyes, strike
with closed fist, hide any weapons in his trunks, or
smear his body with obnoxious chemicals. The referee
is supposed to remind the wrestlers of the rules and
see that they are enforced—if not totally enforced, at
least in spirit. The referee is the sole judge in wrestling, and unless one wrestler pins another's shoulders
to the mat for three seconds, or one makes the other
give up in pain, the referee has to decide who wins the
fall. In boxing the one who wins the most out of ten,
twelve, or fifteen rounds is named the winner; in wrestling it's the one who wins the best out of three falls.
The sheriff had to give the first fall to the Angel. If
there was going to be a third fall, he had to give the
second one to Panzer and the Baron.

What the Baron had to do was stay out of trouble,
and what the Angel had to do was follow Karp's orders
and not hurt them until the third fall. For a while the
Baron did so well the crowd thought there might be a
chance for a pin. Claudius's plan, simple as it was, even
had a chance of working when the Angel let the Baron

catch him in a headlock and the Baron twisted his neck around and ground his nose into a dead-smelling armpit. When the fumes started stinging his eyes, the Angel broke the hold with an off-balance, left-handed smash to the side of the Baron's head. He got out of it, but not before the bug spray did its work. The Angel's eyes were on fire, and the first thing he knew, the Baron had him on his back on the mat, trying to get the pin. The sheriff was down on his hands and knees, feeling for contact between shoulders and mat. "Onetwothree!" Claudius was yelling. "Onetwothree!" He counted to three twice before the sheriff got past two, and by that time it was too late. The Angel flipped the Baron off his shoulders like a gorilla flips a monkey and was on his feet before the sheriff said "three."

Claudius ripped the Stetson off his head and stomped it flat. Karp had two buckets of water at ringside for just such emergencies as foreign chemicals in the eyes. He called his wrestler to him and sloshed him down with both buckets, drenching the Angel and that whole corner of the ring. With the stink gone, the Angel took the offensive. He grabbed the Baron by the leg and started wringing it like an old sock.

At that point the Baron might have yielded to the pain and cried uncle, but Panzer saved him by jumping the ropes and kicking the Angel in the back of the head. Twice more that happened, the Angel threatening to win and Panzer making raids in to save the

Baron's hide. The third time it happened, the Angel didn't just chase Panzer out of the ring; he chased him out of the arena, right out the main gate. While that was going on, the bell rang and the fall ended. Since the Baron was the only one around, the sheriff held up his hands for attention and pointed to the Baron and Panzer's corner to signal that he was awarding the second fall to them.

"The second fall goes to the home folks," Durwood told his listening audience. "It seemed like an awfully quick bell to me, but you know how time flies when you're having fun."

It was some fun, all right. Claudius was *sitting* on his hat by that time, pulling hair out of the back of his head with both hands.

"I think my leg is gone," the Baron said. Rose rubbed his leg with rubbing alcohol and chopped it with the sides of her hands.

"I can't keep my hands from shaking." Panzer held up his right hand to show what he meant, and the hand shook like a slight case of the palsy.

There were only a couple of swallows of pain-killer left in Brothers's bottle, and Claudius, considering where it was needed the most, drank it himself.

The third fall was mercifully short. Durwood Henry got the folks at home ready for it by telling them about the rule changes. "This is it, the moment we've been waiting for, to see if Panzer Kaufman and the Baron can manage to beat a man who's never been bested by anybody. Louis Karp, the Angel's manager, has asked that the rules be suspended so the Angel can keep his vow to beat both wrestlers at the same time. There's no holds barred and no time limit. That means nobody can be saved by the bell or anything else. It's truth-or-consequences time here at the Constance M. Gains Memorial Arena, and it's just about to start."

Karp prepared the Angel by whispering in his ear. "I want you to hurt 'em this time. You understand? It's okay to hurt 'em."

The Angel of Sorrow tried those words in his mind. "Hurt them. Okay to hurt them."

They spent a few minutes stalking each other, the two smaller men harassing the bigger one, cutting in from the rear or flank to grab an arm, a leg, a throat, and getting thrown off or retreating. The attacks could never be coordinated, however, no matter who went first; the Baron was always a count too fast or Panzer was too blamed slow. The Baron once had the Angel's arm twisted in an armlock, but Panzer couldn't get the other arm. The Angel with one arm was just as dangerous as the Angel with two.

The end of the match came after the sparring. The

Baron and Panzer decided they couldn't keep rushing the ape; every time they came back from one of the off-time charges, they had brand-new hickeys on brand-new parts of their bodies. They made the next most dangerous move, a direct frontal attack with both of them going in high. The Angel gave them each a shivering whop in the middle of their foreheads with the heels of his right and left hands. For lesser men than Panzer and the Baron, the match would've been over then and there, but these were two crusty old pros, and they were able to turn the situation to their advantage. They pretended to be hurt worse than they were by instinct, and simultaneously, like two little babies learning to walk, they toddled into their proud mother's arms. The next thing anybody knew, Panzer and the Baron had the Angel's arms twisted high above his back and were running him headfirst into the corner where the steel post was and the soft padding wasn't. The sound of that bald head against that steel post gave five innocent people in the crowd headaches and gave nine children a psychic discomfort that would trouble their dreams later in life.

There was a knot rising on the Angel's head, and those at ringside who could see the Angel's face could see his eyeballs rolling, but somehow he kept his feet.

Claudius was trying to put his flat and badly mangled hat back on his head and yelling at the top of his lungs.

"Don't get overconfident! Finish him off! Finish him off!"

The Baron and Panzer got the Angel by the arms again and backed him tenderly to the middle of the ring for a running start. Showmen to the end, they gave the crowd one final thrill (and Claudius one terrifying fright) by letting go of the Angel's arms, spitting on their hands and wiping them on their trunks, and taking better and stronger grips on the Angel's wrists. When they started the run to the target, there were people in the crowd with their eyes closed and their ears covered. Those who were watching, like Claudius and Squint, saw the Angel snap out of his daze, plant his feet and legs in the mat like pillars on a bridge, and smash Panzer and the Baron together body to body like cymbals. They came to rest on their backs on the canvas. They looked almost peaceful as they lay with the soles of their feet touching; the only thing missing was a flock of chirping bluebirds circling their heads.

"Didn't I tell you not to get overconfident?" Claudius was moaning. "Didn't I say that?"

The Angel of Sorrow still had to hold one of the sleeping wrestler's shoulders down to the count of three, but there wasn't any doubt that the match was over.

30: Claudius the Philosopher

The kitchen that night was a quiet place. The Baron and Panzer had lost the match, so naturally they felt bad. Betty and Rose weren't happy because their men, both covered with glowing rainbows of whelps and bruises, weren't happy. The Marked Marvel and the Claw weren't in the best of spirits either, 'cause unless there suddenly came a miracle, they were the Angel's next victims.

Claudius was the only one who was even remotely happy, and that's not saying much. His boys had lost, and his best ten-gallon hat was a shambles, and he'd pulled more hair out of his head than he could afford, but otherwise, things couldn't be better. Between the money they'd collected from the ticket sales and the money they'd made at the concession stand, they now had $4,000. Things were going so well that if only a thousand people showed up for the next two matches, they'd still be able to pay the bank.

"You know, boys," he said, looking up from the stacks of money on the table in front of him, "except for a few sore places here and there, the hardest part is almost over." The Mask and the Claw didn't believe it was over. "I mean," Claudius went on, "we got the bank note made, and we're gonna make plenty extra for ourselves. We've only got one small problem left to take care of; then we're set up for life."

The wrestlers were too tired and didn't have the energy to argue with him over his use of the word "small." If the Angel of Sorrow was a small problem, they didn't want to spend the night with a big one. And Rose was a bit on the shy side when it came to speaking up for herself, but Betty wasn't. "You're dreaming if you think my Panzer is gonna git back in the ring with that animal. What good's the rest of your life if somebody's got to roll you around in a wheelchair?"

Julie imagined her sweet Masked Marvel being hurt. She closed her eyes and saw him wrapped up like a mummy in the hospital, his arms and legs in those traction swings and pulleys, his whole body wrapped up right to the edge of his purple and black mask, those horrible tubes going in his mouth and nose.

"Ain't nobody gonna get hurt," Claudius said. He could sense their reluctance to believe him, but he wouldn't be much of a promoter if he couldn't reassure people that he was right about their lives and money. He took out a cigar, licked it up till it was soggy, leaned back in his chair, and lit it. "Let's ask ourselves, 'What does the Angel want?' "

"The Angel don't want nothing," Betty said. "I seen the look in his eyes, and he ain't smart enough to want nothing."

"That's right," Claudius said, being truthful. "It's

not the Angel that's the brains behind that outfit. Karp's the one we're dealing with, and Karp can be had."

"So what does Karp want?" Betty said, not letting Claudius get out of his argument that easily.

"What do we all want if it ain't money? The thing about money is, the less we have, the more we want, and the more we got, the more we want. You see how it works? Everybody wants something, and most people want money. But it doesn't matter what you want, there's always somebody or something there to keep you from getting it. Now hasn't it always been that way?"

Everybody thought about it, and they had to agree Claudius was right and telling the truth again.

"It's been that way ever since time began, now hasn't it?"

They had to agree it had.

"Well, that's what I'm talking about," he said. "It's like a real-life wrestling match: You're trying to get a hold on somebody, and somebody's always trying to get a hold on you. You're trying to get them to give up and give you what you want, and they're out to do the same thing to you; now ain't that the truth?"

Nobody would've disagreed on the point so far.

"So this is what I mean: There ain't no such thing as a hold you can't get out of, now is there?"

"There's the Chinese Backbreaker," Panzer said, and

the others agreed. Nobody had ever broken the Chinese Backbreaker, and that was a fact.

"And there's the Japanese Sleeper," the Baron said, and that too was true.

Claudius knew about those holds. "That's right," he said, thinking, "but using those holds in a wrestling match is like using a shotgun. I mean, there are some things that aren't really wrestling. I mean, there ain't no *legal* hold that can't be reversed, so you see what we've got to do."

They didn't see.

"We've got to let Karp think he's got us where we can't escape, and then we've got to spring our reverse." Claudius let that sink in awhile. Then he told them, "Right now we're all in the middle of what looks like a hot summer, but on the other side of the world right now, down in Argentina and Brazil, they're getting ready for a hard winter. And right now we're all getting ready to go to bed, but over in China they're just getting out of bed to go to work. Think of that. What's happening to them right now won't happen to us until tomorrow."

Squint hadn't said anything, only watched and listened, and he found himself amazed at how easy his father led the others along.

"So you see," Claudius finished, "nobody has anything to worry about. All you two guys got to do is wrestle with the Angel." He looked at the Mask and the Claw. "And all I've got to do is take care of Karp. Karp, right now, is right where I want him. He thinks he's got *us* right where he wants, and that's what we want him to think."

Somehow or another, using nothing but cigar smoke and heartfelt words, Claudius convinced them that everything was going to be fine, and that's what Claudius had intended to do. He'd given them so many things to think about—the Chinaman getting out of bed, Karp playing right into their hands and all—that nobody asked him to explain how he had Karp where he wanted him, and nobody remembered how it was *them* getting in the ring with the Angel, not Claudius.

"Lean on my shoulder, sugar," Rose told her Baron. "I'll help you get up the stairs."

They all went off peacefully to bed, everybody, that is, except Julie and the Mask, who wanted to sit for a while in the front porch swing, and Squint and Claudius, who lingered in the kitchen for a few minutes, not really looking at each other.

Both of them knew the same thing: The thing they needed most was an idea, and Claudius didn't have one. Claudius looked at his son and said, "Well?"

Squint didn't have anything to say because he didn't have an idea either. That's the way they went to bed, thinking.

31: Trouble Makes the Heart Grow Fonder

The Masked Marvel and Julie were in love. Anybody who'd been watching over the last few days could have seen it; since the wrestling crew came back from their exhibition in Dallas, the two of them had been inseparable. Holding hands. Looking at each other all the time. Swinging in the swing. That kind of thing.

In the morning they were off together to check the mail, walking down to the mailbox on the main road. Ordinarily it takes about five minutes to walk to get the mail, the newspaper, or whatever's down there. The way they were walking, it was gonna take an hour. They were taking baby steps, kicking clods of dirt, backing up, walking sideways, kicking more clods, and talking.

Squint watched them from the top of the bleachers till he couldn't stand it anymore.

If he could've heard what they were saying, he wouldn't have wanted to listen either.

"I never want too much," Julie was saying. "Just the things everybody wants. I like to cook, and sew, and sit in the swing when it's hot, and I like to ride in cars. I like animals, and kids, and I'd like someday to have my own house. I wouldn't grow potatoes, I'll tell you that; I'd grow flowers in the summer and move them inside in the winter. I think I'd like a green-house."

"You like kids, huh?" the Mask asked. He wouldn't mind having five or six, but more than that, he thought, might be too many.

Then she had a sad look on her face, and he thought he'd said something wrong.

He hadn't. "I just don't like to think about you getting hurt," Julie said.

He was glad that what he did for a living was dangerous, more than glad. He liked having somebody worry about him, and besides Claudius and the Claw, who didn't count because they were men and his friends, there hadn't been anybody.

"There's always a chance that you may get hurt," the Mask said. "Wrestling's just like that. But you eat good, and you get plenty of exercise and plenty of sleep, so you keep in pretty good shape." He tried to explain how most of the time one wrestler knew what another one was going to do, and when you were in good shape and practiced, somebody could lift you over his head and slam you down on your back and it wouldn't hurt.

"Watch me fall," he said, and he jumped in the air right beside her, swung his legs straight out in front of his body, and came down flat on his back in the road. The dust flew everywhere, and there was a loud whump, but he was smiling. The back of his pants, shirt, and mask were covered, but it was the kind of dust that was like baby powder, and all you had to do to get rid of it was shake it off.

If Squint had seen that, the Mask jumping up in the air like a lunatic madman and falling on his back, he wouldn't have known what to think. Luckily he was busy picking up trash in the arena and didn't see it. He had a sawed-off broomstick with a nail in the end and was spearing drink cups, hot dog wrappers, and empty peanut bags under the seats. He also had his eye out for dropped money, and right when the Mask was throwing himself on the ground like a man possessed, Squint was picking up his third quarter. Right after that he saw a whole dollar bill in the grass. There's something about seeing a dollar bill like that, something that makes you have to stop and catch your breath. Finding money borders on complete happiness.

At the same time Squint was finding money under the bleachers, birds, sparrows and wrens, were singing cheerfully on the power line that ran from the top of the billboards down to the front porch. Claudius came out the front door with a cup of coffee in one hand and a can of beer in the other; he looked at the morning and the birds and shook the wire to run them off.

"When you're on the road a lot," the Mask was saying, "you wrestle in places where it's a lot better to let the local heroes win. The safest part of wrestling is what goes on in the ring; most of the time, it's the crowd you're worried about." He tried to explain. "The crowd is everything. They've got to be heated up because it's their money that keeps everything going, but you can get them too heated. Once over in Odessa the Claw had Ranger Ralph on the ropes and was choking him with his hook, not too hard, you know, 'cause the Ranger was going to win the fall anyway, and a woman on the front row pulled out this pearl-handled pistol and pointed it at the Claw's head and told him, 'Let 'im go, you cheating freak, or you're gonna have another claw, right between the eyes.' What made it worse was Ranger Ralph, who was drunk, telling the woman to go ahead and shoot."

Julie didn't like the idea of him getting hurt and told him so. She wasn't sure she even liked wrestling.

"Aw," he said, "most of the time the worst you've got to look out for is little old ladies with hatpins."

Quit wrestling?

"I'm the Masked Marvel," he said. "How could I ever quit wrestling?"

Under ordinary circumstances, Squint would've used the money he found to pay his way into twelve movies, or eight movies if he bought popcorn. The way it used to be, when his mother was the boss, to go to the picture shows, you had to sneak off or say you were going to play or go fishing. Movies were one of the things the devil used to tempt people, Constance believed, unless they were good movies like *Samson and Delilah*. For some crazy reason it was all right to watch Samson kill off thousands and thousands of Philistines, but it wasn't right to see John Wayne knocking off Indians and Japs.

If you ever found any money, the dumbest thing you could do was tell Constance about it 'cause Constance would make you put it in the offering plate that Sunday; you could count on it. And nothing looked worse than a whole dollar bill in the offering plate. Once they landed there, they were gone forever.

Claudius was not in the best mood when he finished his beer and sipped his coffee. During the night he'd dreamed a dark dream, one where he was riding in a rowboat in some kind of mossy swamp in Louisiana, and the Angel of Sorrow was doing the rowing, taking him someplace where he didn't want to go. It was the kind of dream where you know it is a dream, and you keep telling the Angel, "This ain't nothing but a dream. You can't scare nobody," and you keep telling yourself, "I can wake up anytime I want." Only you don't wake up because you're curious about where he is taking you. The Angel never says where he's taking you; all he does is look at you with a look that's kind of satisfied and hungry at the same time. The thing that had Claudius mad was that he never got to find out where the Angel was taking him. The last thing he remembered was falling asleep in the boat.

The night had also failed to provide him with any inspiration as to how to get out of the fix he was in. Neither had it inspired any of his wrestlers. The Baron woke up with his leg so stiff and sore Rose had to go to town to get him some crutches. Panzer was wearing a patty of hamburger meat in a bandage over the left side of his forehead to try to get the swelling to go down; from his ankles to his armpits, he was fuming with liniment.

The Baron and Panzer hobbled out to the porch and sat in the swing. The flies kept trying to swarm around Panzer's hamburger meat bandage, but the smell of his body kept making them crash. They crashed into the side of the house and the screen and into the Baron, who was too tired and sore to finish them off.

"Pitiful," Claudius said, "just plain pitiful."

Squint crawled out from under the bleachers and pulled his sack of gathered trash after him. He'd filled a burlap bag and crammed it even fuller and in the process found a grand total of $1.91. Quietly he gave the money to Claudius, his offering to the growing account.

Waiting for them in the mailbox were the morning newspaper and a small pink envelope addressed to Julie. She opened it and found an invitation to a birthday dance being given the coming Saturday night for one of her former classmates, a blond cheerleader named Tanya Tobey. Julie's assigned escort for the dance was the short, chubby captain of the basketball team, Mr. Personality, Jeff Rowe.

She read the invitation and put it back in the envelope, but not before the Mask had seen it and recognized it for what it was.

"Don't look so sad," she said. "I'm not going."

The Mask did indeed look sad. You couldn't see anything except his eyes, but they looked like the poor little baby raccoon's in the Prevent Forest Fires poster, the one whose home has been burned. He didn't like the idea of her going to the dance with somebody else, and he didn't like her missing out on fun because of him. "They invited you," he told her. "I think you ought to go."

She thought about it as they started back. "I'll go if you go as my date," she decided, but her decision didn't make the Mask any happier.

"Aw, I'm not anybody to dance with," he said.

She thought about it again. "You don't know how to dance, do you?"

Under his mask the Mask was blushing. He'd always wanted to learn to dance but never dreamed that anybody'd ever want to teach him and so had ruled out even wanting to dance. He'd always been too big, too used to moving heavier things with his body than a girl. He was six feet tall and weighed well over two hundred pounds; a girl hardly weighed more than a feather duster . . . what would happen if he ever stepped on one of her feet?

"I'll teach you to dance," Julie said, almost pulling him along toward the front gate. "You teach me to wrestle."

Squint watched them come into the arena and climb in the ring. Claudius watched, too, but he didn't have near the terrible thoughts that Squint did. It was as though the whole, horrible future was flashing before his eyes; he could see a clothesline with clothes blowing in the Texas wind—a man's pair of pants, a dress, a bunch of cotton diapers, and three baby-sized Masked Marvel masks.

"I suppose she could have picked worse," Claudius said, philosophizing again.

Squint closed his eyes and tried to imagine how it could be worse, and the only thing he could think of was three little babies with steel hooks on their arms.

The Mask and Julie were in their own world. They were in the middle of the ring with their arms around each other and their heads rubbing on each other's shoulders, and though they weren't doing anything, exactly, just moving around in place, it looked like they were about to do something, and nobody on the porch was sure what was coming next. Betty and Rose came out and watched for a minute, then started fussing at the three men and Squint for watching.

There was a commotion as the women tried to get their husbands out of the swing and into the house, and the commotion caused the very thing the women wanted to avoid. The Mask and Julie came back to earth and saw that they were being watched. They let go and jumped back from each other so quick they almost caused a breeze, but it was too late. They'd been seen.

"What in the world were you two doing, if you don't mind my asking?" Claudius asked. Julie and the Mask had come to the porch to face the music.

"Wrestling," the Mask said at the exact same time Julie said, "Dancing," and you'd have thought the two were going to melt into their shoes. There wasn't any way they could've explained it, and there wasn't any doubt in the minds of those who'd seen it. The Masked

Marvel and Julie Gains were in love.

The Baron and Rose, Panzer and Betty, and even Squint found something appropriate to do elsewhere in the house.

Claudius sat on the edge of the porch with his feet dangling over the side, looking at the birds that had shown up again on the wire.

32: A Pot of Chili, a Can of Beans, a Quiet Meal, a Hunk of Ham

By afternoon the sun was doing its damnedest to bake the brains out of the earth and every creature that walked on it. There wasn't any place to get relief except deep under the front porch, dug down in the musky dirt with the cool stone walls of the cellar against your back, but Seymour had claimed that spot for himself and wasn't about to be rooted out.

It was a Wednesday, and on Wednesdays radio station KRIT put on a show called *Championship Chili* where a bona fide chili cook cooked up a pot of chili on the radio, giving his recipe as he went along so folks at home could copy it and make their own. Half the people in East Texas would be eating chili that night, no, more than half; the only way to beat the heat was to get the heat inside your body, and there wasn't any better way to do that than with chili.

Constance Gains had been against the eating of chili on the grounds that it contributed to immoral and sinful behavior, especially among men. It had been Claudius's favorite food, and that was proof enough. For six years she'd refused to let Herman cook it, and he'd had to listen to the radio show recipes without being able to try any. Finally, he was getting his chance, and he was in the kitchen, cooking along.

The guest chef on that Wednesday's show was a Mexican-American named Juan Carlos Jose de Ramirez, a short, fuzzy-headed, wild-eyed fellow who had the nickname *Toro poco de las Mesa,* or in English, Little Bull of the Table or Small Bull of the High Plateau, depending on how you translated it. As he gave his recipe in Spanish, a somewhat bilingual Texas voice translated.

"I like hot chili, very hot, so I use six peppers to feed twelve people. I must warn you to be careful to use less, as they do not call me the Little Bull of the Table for nothing."

"Juan Carlos says he likes his chili hot, and he's putting in the peppers, six of the meanest-looking rascals I've ever seen in my life. They're about as long and skinny as your grandmother's little finger, and they've got the color of baked chicken beaks. You-all know what baked chicken beaks look like, don't you?"

Herman was listening to the radio and cooking along. In his head he was figuring out how many people he might have to feed: Squint, Julie, Claudius, himself, the Baron, Panzer, Betty, Rose, the Claw, the Mask, the two wrestlers who were coming in for the first match, the sheriff maybe, and maybe a few others. The wrestlers would eat as much as three normal people, so he was figuring Juan Carlos's recipe for forty-eight, cooking it in a kettle big enough to wash clothes. Four times six peppers was twenty-four peppers, which he poured in from a discolored jar he kept under the sink, holding his face averted to avoid the fumes.

The next set of instructions from Juan Carlos concerned garlic and onions, of which he used an ample supply and Herman used four times as much. "Uh, Juan Carlos says to put in all the garlic and onions you want, the more the better, because garlic and onions carry a strong aroma and make it irresistible for everybody within smelling distance," the Texas voice said. The smelling distance for what Herman was cooking was about three square miles.

Which, of course, included the little travel trailer parked in the side yard where the Angel of Sorrow and Karp were.

The closer it got to suppertime, the more irresistible the smell coming in their window was going to be.

"You know what they're trying to do, don't you?" Karp said.

The Angel sat at the little table in the kitchenette area of the trailer in front of the fan and said nothing.

"They're trying to get to us, but they ain't going to."

Karp was sitting on the couch in the living-room area of the trailer, barefooted, flipping cards one at a time from a deck at his boots. He got up after missing three in a row and closed the window to keep the good smell out and the bad smell in. Then he turned on a burner on the stove and started heating a can of pork and beans. It wasn't a regular can of beans, but one of the giant economy sizes that restaurants buy to feed a whole day's customers, and there were about twenty empty cans the same size stacked up and festering in the corner.

"You know what this means?" Karp said, returning to the couch and taking a slip of paper from his shirt pocket. The Angel lifted his eyelids and looked, again without saying anything. It wasn't anything but a piece of newspaper.

Then Karp took a dollar bill from his wallet and held it up alongside the newspaper to show that they were the same size. "This means they ain't got the money. It means everything they got now is gonna be ours after tomorrow night, after you finish them off. It means just keep doing like we're doing; just keep doing what I tell you, and we'll be eating that chili and they'll be eating this slop."

The Angel thought about chili; then he looked at the can of beans on the stove and at the empty cans stacked in the corner. He didn't say anything; he just looked slow and steady at Karp, and he thought about the chili cooking in that big house, and he looked at those beans again.

Herman had guessed right, sure enough, about the sheriff's showing up in time for supper. He'd only a moment before called his eaters into the kitchen and put bowls in their hands and got them lined up in front of the kettle where he could serve them chili when the sheriff came in with the results of a search he'd made for Claudius.

The lawman opened a leather pouch he was carrying and took out handfuls of WANTED posters, some of them with big headlines, "WANTED—DEAD OR ALIVE," and pitched them on the table. "I went through everything," the sheriff said, "and unfortunately the Angel ain't there." He took out a pad from his back pocket and looked at it.

"I also wired the FBI and the Texas Rangers in Austin and the state police boys in Baton Rouge, in Jackson, Mississippi, and in Albany, up there in New York. There wasn't any warrants out for his arrest, so

far as they could tell, though they all know the Angel
and Karp. It seems the Angel and Karp stir things up
everywhere they go, especially in Jackson."

"What happened in Jackson?" Claudius wanted to
know.

The sheriff took off his hat and scratched his head
thoughtfully. "Well, it seems the sheriff of Hinds
County over there has got a brother-in-law that wres-
tles part time and runs a school bus for the county
when he's not wrestling. . . ." He looked at the Mask
and the Claw like he was sorry to have to tell them
what he was about to tell them. "It seems he wrestled
the Angel one time, and the Angel started swinging
him around by the hair, swinging him like he wasn't
nothing but a rag doll, and his hair popped loose from
his skull. They say it made a kind of sucking sound
like when you stick a glass on your mouth and pull it
off. Say now when you rub your hand over the brother-
in-law's head, it feels like the back of the neck of a bird
dog, all wrinkled wavy. . . ."

The Claw and the Mask were awfully glad he told
them that.

"Sheriff in Jackson says if we hold the Angel a few
days, his brother-in-law'll be down here to snuff him
out."

The sheriff knew what Claudius was thinking and
said, "I can't do it. First of all, *I'd* have to arrest 'im,

and he might not want to go. Second of all, the jail wouldn't hold him. And if that ain't enough, I got an election coming up, and I ain't no spring chicken anymore."

Claudius handed the sheriff a cold beer for his trouble, and Herman handed him an empty bowl, and Sheriff Jernigen got in the chili line with the others.

One by one they stepped up to the stove, and Herman filled their bowls. Squint was the last in line, and he noticed that they all looked in the pot when it was their turn, almost like checking to see what they were up against. The closer they got to the front, the bigger their bowls seemed to be getting, like a bunch of kids lined up for their typhoid shots; the closer you get to the needle, the bigger that needle gets. When Herman filled them up, they carried their bowls to the table like they were transporting hot lava.

Nobody took a bite until everybody was served, and then they didn't exactly dig in.

"Shore smells good," Panzer said, passing his nose dangerously close to the steaming concoction.

"Shore does," a few of the others said. Their noses were all busy, but their spoons were all resting, and nobody took a bite till Claudius did.

He took a bite. He chewed it and swallowed it down and smiled. He looked completely innocent, like he was wondering why everybody was watching him eat and not eating. Then everybody took a bite, and there was a general sigh of relief or resignation around the table.

The first bite wasn't nothing, Squint thought, and he too had looked in the pot at that scalding sludge. The second bite wasn't hardly anything either; it might be a little bit on the warm side, but it was still delicious. On the third bite he noticed that the room seemed to be cooling off. On the fourth spoonful, it hit him, just when it hit all the others. His eyes began to water, and he put his spoon down and looked around the table. The Mask was popping his mask against his head, Julie and the sheriff were guzzling down water, Betty and Rose were fanning their mouths, and the Claw was banging his hook against the table.

The only ones who didn't seem to be suffering from the heat in their throats and bellies were Claudius and Herman, who got up to refill their bowls.

Squint poured some water in his mouth, and he could have sworn it sizzled. His mouth was in flames, just like he'd just eaten asphalt, but the heat came in waves, and if you waited till things cooled down, you could take another bite and stir them up again. It was just like eating ice cream, only in reverse. The secret was not to eat too fast, and as soon as he learned that, he felt he'd joined a club, a special club of chili eaters, made up mostly of men. He finished the whole bowl, and Claudius, he thought, was proud of him.

Squint was exactly right in thinking Claudius was proud of him. Claudius would've been disappointed if his own son had acted like a baby or a little old lady who was afraid of anything a little hot. And Squint was right in feeling he'd joined a club. The club didn't have a name, but it had a code of honor, which was something like the Code of the West. Everybody knew what it was, but nobody could put it into words.

Constance was also right with her suspicion that chili contributed to sin. She, more than anyone else, understood the corrupting effect that chili worked on people and the power it had. A case in point was what happened next, the arrival of Ranger Ralph Travis and Hog Jarvis.

They had finished eating and Claudius had called them all to the front porch to plan that night's activity when the main gate opened and in walked two men carrying suitcases. The bigger man, over six feet tall and lanky, was carrying the smaller suitcase, and he was something to look at. He was wearing a big white cowboy hat that was so white it stung your eyes to look at it. He had a face below the hat that was as weatherbeaten as an old tin roof, like hot sun didn't mean any more to him than it did to a lizard. The closer he came to the porch, the easier it was to see that he was a real man, a rugged West Texas bullslinger. Below the face was a fringed red and gold cowboy outfit something like the kind Roy Rogers wore in the movies. On his shirt pocket was a six-pointed ranger's star with little tin balls covering the points, and in the center of the star were his picture and name spelled out, "Ranger Ralph," like an autograph. On his hips he was wearing a matching set of pearl-handled six-guns.

The other man, Hog Jarvis, was wearing overalls and loose, flopping clodhopper boots. His thick hair, black as used motor oil, was braided in pigtails that hung to his waist and were tucked under a rope that was tied around his middle. His body was S-shaped under the traveling trunk he carried on his back. When he got to the porch and swung the trunk down, his back was still S-shaped.

"Ranger Ralph Travis and Hog Jarvis," Claudius introduced them, and the wrestlers of the house greeted the newcomers as brothers.

The Ranger snapped open his suitcase and pulled out a Ranger Ralph badge like the one he wore on his shirt. He handed it to Squint and said, "There you go, buckaroo; now you're deputized as a member in good standing of the Ranger Ralph Club. Wear it proudly, and always take good care of it 'cause one of these days it's gonna be a collector's item."

Squint had just about decided that there wasn't a wrestler anywhere that was completely sane and normal when Hog Jarvis started snorting like a hog, tugging on the Ranger's shirt sleeve, and jumping up and down. "SNNNNNNORK, SNNNNOERK, SNNNNNNORK," he said, excited.

Ranger Ralph seemed to understand the hog talk and cocked his nose in the air. He took a deep smell through his nose, thought about it for a second, then took another deep sniff. "Hot dog if you ain't right," he said, pulling his guns. "That's championship chili!"

He shot both pistols three times in the air and started up the steps with the Hog right behind him, hot stepping it to the source of the aroma, serious eating on their minds.

Under the porch Seymour was so scared he was trying to claw his way through the cellar stones.

33: Squint Takes a Chance

Again they came. Again they came in cars and trucks, by ambulance and taxi, on horses, mules, and tractors. They even came by chartered Trailways all the way from Darco, Waskom, and Leigh, where word of the matches had spread. Many families brought picnic baskets and ate supper in their seats in the stands, chicken salad sandwiches, chocolate pies, and butter-milk. It was Squint's first duty of the night to pass among them, selling Ranger Ralph badges and pen-ants. He also passed out leaflets with the address where they could send for complete Ranger Ralph outfits, Ranger Ralph hats and shirts, and Ranger Ralph cap guns. The Ranger didn't leave too many stones un-turned when it came to fame and money.

Squint's second duty was to carry the flag again, this time in a little white sailor suit in honor of the men and boys who gave their lives at sea. If there was an army of souls up there in heaven, Claudius reasoned, there had to be a navy, too, and it was only good busi-ness to dedicate a night to them the same as he had the Army.

The opening ceremony went off better than before; at least the record didn't skip. Just before they were introduced to the audience in the arena, the Ranger and Hog had a few words for those listening at home.

The Hog gomped and snorted, squeezing air back and forth around the bottom of his nose.

"He's saying hello to all his friends in Springdale, Arkansas, his mother and father and his girl friend, Rhonda Jean," the Ranger translated.

The Hog snorted again, and Ranger Ralph cut in. "He's mighty glad there's people out there listening, and he wants me to remind you all that we got Ranger

Ralph Club badges, and hats, and outfits for sale, and if you're interested in owning anything in the Ranger Ralph line of western wear, the address to write is Ranger Ralph, Post Office Box One-oh-nine, that's Post Office Box One-oh-nine, Del Rio, Texas. . . ."

When Squint finished with the flag, he was through with all duties till intermission after the first fall of the second fight, when he had to take Seymour around. Claudius ran the arena like a circus, and everybody knew when he was on.

Squint was in his bedroom changing clothes when he heard a loud yell, a genuine rebel yell, coming from the arena. Ranger Ralph and the Hog was in the ring, and it was the Ranger's war cry that was making all the noise. The Ranger's ring outfit included a fringed white leather vest, white trunks, and his matching six-guns. Before the sheriff made him take them off, he pulled them and started shooting at the Hog's feet, making him do the hog dance. Squint didn't see how anybody in the arena or anybody listening at home could have much doubt about who was going to win the match. You just knew the Ranger was gonna strangle the Hog in his own hair.

Nor could there be much doubt who was going to win the second match either. It would take ten Masked Marvels and Steel Claws to beat the Angel of Sorrow, and then maybe ten wouldn't be enough. When a few moments later Squint looked out the side window to the yard and saw Karp walking from the trailer toward the main gate, he decided to take a chance.

He turned off the kitchen light and slipped out through the screen door to the back porch. The lights from the arena reflected the dust in the air and gave an eerie glow to the dry, crusty piece of the farm between the house and the trailer. Still, it was possible for a body to stick low to the ground, move like a cat, and not be noticed. And that's what Squint had in mind, to sneak a look in the trailer window and learn something maybe. He didn't have to worry about being quiet; the racket of the crowd in the arena covered the sound of his movements. He zigzagged left and right toward the light coming from the crack in the window to the left of the trailer door.

Without being seen, he made it to the darkness below the window and rested. If Karp came back suddenly, Squint's plan was to jump under the trailer, crawl through to the other side, and hightail it back to the house, but his immediate plan was to get a look inside the trailer.

He watched the direction in which Karp had gone and saw nothing. He listened intently, but all he could hear was the muted noise of the arena and the drone scratching of the grasshoppers and crickets. It was now or never, he decided, and he turned to face the trailer and slowly rise to window level. The top of his head cleared the bottom of the crack of light, then his forehead, then his eyes. Instead of looking into the trailer, though, he suddenly found himself looking into the eyes of the Angel of Sorrow.

You might say it scared him a little. It scared every living molecule in his body and brains, and he jumped straight backward like a king rattler had snapped at his face. His heart took a thump he could hear in his ears, but he didn't run. Some instinct inside him told him to hold his ground.

The trailer door swung open slowly, and light spilled out to where he was standing. Then the Angel looked out, and Squint silently prepared to become a corpse, to be a sad story in the newspaper that would make everybody who read it cry. He closed his eyes and imagined the headline: "ANGEL OF SORROW RIPS HEAD AND ARMS OFF BOY 11." He braced himself for the terrible pain, but no pain came, and he slowly opened his eyes.

"You come to spy on me," the Angel said, halfway a question and halfway a fact. His voice sounded like a frog croaking in a foggy cave, but he could talk, and did, and to Squint it was like music on a beautiful day.

"No," Squint said, thinking about as fast as his mind would let him. "I come to see if you want some chili."

Squint didn't know it, but he'd just said the magic words.

"You want to be my friend?" the Angel asked.

The only answer to that question was "Yes."

"Good," the Angel said, smiling. "My name is Arthur."

The chance Squint had taken was about to pay off.

34: Claudius Strikes Another Deal

Claudius and Karp were watching Ranger Ralph and the Hog go at it in the ring. They were in the second fall already, the Hog having taken the first one with his famous hog-wild moves in which he started snorting, grunting, and running around the ring from rope to rope like a wild pig gone crazy, then slamming into the lanky Ranger like a cannonball or more like a giant peeled cantaloupe. Nobody is supposed to be strong enough to survive a hog-wild charge from Hog Jarvis, but somehow the Ranger survived it enough to get up on his shaky legs and be saved by the bell. Now, in the second fall, the Ranger was choking the Hog with the Hog's long hair, not by twisting it around his neck, but by ramming it in his mouth and forcing it down his throat.

"That's a great act," Karp said to Claudius, appreciative.

The crowd was liking it, and for the time being that was all Claudius was concerned about.

"Same deal as last night?" Karp offered. The Angel would fake it for the first two falls and give the crowd its money's worth. In the third fall, well, the third fall would have to be decided by pain. "You do know what pain is, don't you, Colonel?" Karp said, smiling.

The only thing Claudius could do was accept the offer.

"Oh, by the way," Karp said, starting to walk away, then stopping and turning back. He took the piece of money-sized paper from his pocket and handed it to the puzzled and innocent-looking Claudius. "I thought you just might want to know I saw myself a lawyer today, and he asked me an interesting question." Claudius didn't say anything, and Karp didn't expect him to. "Lawyer asked me, 'When everything Gains is got is yours, what you planning to do with it?' and I said, 'I don't know,' and he said, 'Did you ever hear of shopping centers?' Never seen a man more anxious to take a case," Karp finished, smiling at the pain he could read in Claudius's sad eyes.

In the ring the Hog was flat on his belly, moaning, and Ranger Ralph was sitting on the side of the Hog's head, trying to tie one of his arms to one of his legs in a square knot.

35: Karp Makes a Mistake

Karp almost felt like singing. It was a beautiful night, a night to be remembered for years to come. Things couldn't be more perfect as far as he was concerned; the Angel had never been more in control of a situation with so much to gain and so little to lose. The most beautiful thing of all was he himself, Louis A. Karp, the grand architect of the grand design. If anything went wrong now, he'd kiss an alligator lip to lip.

He thought about it. He'd had a hard life in comparison to other people's. He was the kind of man who never argued about rules—rules were made for the lame and inept—and he'd always found a way to get what he wanted or needed. Mostly he let other people make mistakes; then he took advantage of them, and mostly rules worked in his favor.

He listened to the crickets and grasshoppers on the way from the arena to the trailer to start getting the Angel ready, and it was downright hard to suppress a burst of laughter. He couldn't, in fact, suppress it. He started laughing, glad he wasn't Claudius Gains. He was thinking, After all, I didn't do nothing that he wouldn't have done, only I was smarter. That's what he was, he decided, smarter than your average person.

The crickets seemed to be saying his name, *Karrrrrr-*

rrrrrp, Karp, Karp, Karrrrrrrrrrrp.

He rounded the corner of the arena wall and saw the trailer, and saw the Angel sitting on the catwalk, and saw the Gains kid handing the Angel a bowl of something. A cheer broke out behind him in the arena as the first match neared its conclusion; whatever was happening in there wasn't nearly as important as what was happening before his very eyes. The Angel took the bowl the Gains kid gave him and downed it in one gulp. "No!" Karp yelled, but it was too late. He started running toward the trailer and got there just as the heat hit the Angel's mouth, and his wrestler started banging his head against the trailer wall.

"What in hell you doing?" he yelled, reaching the Angel and slapping the empty bowl from his hands. "How do you know that stuff ain't poisoned?"

Karp felt like he had to do the thinking for the whole world sometimes. The Angel was trying to figure out what he'd done wrong.

"That's not just any kid," Karp said, turning to Squint and pointing. "That's the Gains's kid, and you can't trust him any more'n you can trust his old man."

"Arthur and I are friends," Squint said, taking the empty bowl and the unused spoon from the Angel.

"Arthur, is it? Friends, is it?" Karp advanced on the boy, fully intending to give him a good shaking and send him back to his daddy by the scruff of his neck, and he would've done it, except a low, rumbling growl from the Angel stopped him dead in his tracks. "Get out of here, kid," Karp said instead, jerking his thumb in the direction of the arena, "before you get hurt."

Squint didn't need any more coaxing; he left to go back to the arena with the feeling that he had accomplished something, but not knowing what. Before turning the corner to the main gate, he looked behind him at the Angel and waved. He couldn't be sure in that half-light, but he thought he saw the Angel give a little wave back; that alone would have been an accomplishment.

The Angel sat on the catwalk steps by the door of the trailer, and Karp stuffed both hands in the baggy pockets of his green suit pants and sat down beside him.

"I can see right now I made a mistake," Karp said, "leaving you out here alone. Suppose there'd been knockout drops in that stuff he gave you, you'd be asleep right now, and where would we be?"

"Aw," the Angel said, "he wouldn't do nothing like that."

"But we don't know, do we? My biggest mistake was not locking you up. Every time I don't, you get in trouble."

They could hear then the ring bell clanging wildly above the roaring of the crowd. The first match was over, and the Angel focused his dim intelligence on the work he was about to be called on to do. "I ain't gonna hurt nobody," he said, his lower lip puffed out in defiance of anything Karp might say. "And you can't make me."

Karp could see the damage that Squint had done and wisely didn't try. "Arthur," he said gently, "you don't have to hurt anybody. You don't have to do anything you don't want to, but you have to win. You understand that, don't you? You have to win."

Karp explained what would happen if they didn't win while the Angel flexed his muscles and loosened up for the ring. If the Angel didn't beat those clowns, they'd have to sell the trailer and sleep on the ground. They wouldn't even be able to buy the beans they'd been eating.

36: Claudius Also Makes a Mistake

The Masked Marvel was pacing back and forth in front of the pool table in the living room; the Claw was sitting at the bar, sharpening the point of his hook. Claudius, Panzer, and the Baron were slouched in chairs, trying to think of something.

"Tell me about those two illegal holds," Claudius said, fishing for ideas.

Panzer told him about the Chinese Backbreaker, where you stood across your opponent's back while he was lying facedown on the mat, and you pulled his legs up behind him and hooked his feet up under your arms. "The trouble with the backbreaker is," Panzer lamented, "it's impossible to get on anybody."

The Baron told them about the Japanese Sleeper, where you stood directly behind your opponent with your left arm across his throat and your left hand holding onto your right elbow; your right elbow is across your opponent's shoulder where your left hand can grab it; your right hand is behind your opponent's head, pushing it forward.

He showed them how to get the hold then, demonstrating on the Claw. He had the Claw stand in front of him face to face, then spun him around in his shoes almost with a straight-arm in the shoulder. With the Claw turned in the right direction, the Baron's forearm was in perfect position to get the hold. He got it, and in less than five seconds the Claw was asleep.

"Now why didn't we think of that last night?" Claudius asked, but what was there to say? You couldn't think of something before you thought of something, and nobody had thought of it till now.

The Baron laid the Claw down gently on the living-room floor; then they lifted him to the pool table and watched for consciousness to return.

"How long's he gonna be that way?" Claudius asked.

The Baron answered four or five minutes.

While the Claw was still out, Squint came in.

He told them how he'd been to the trailer and talked to the Angel, how he'd peeked in the window and been eyeball to eyeball with him, and how the Angel had come out and made friends, how his name was Arthur, and how he was mean only because Karp made him be.

"And you believed him?" Claudius asked. Squint said that he did, and Claudius made his decision. "Well, I don't," he said. "Human life don't mean any more to him than buzzard life, and if we don't get him, he's gonna get us."

The Claw moaned and began to rejoin the living as a loud chorus of boos and catcalls told them the Angel was coming into the arena and climbing in the ring. The Claw got up from the pool table and began to clear his head.

"Okay, here's the plan," Claudius said, in his mind weighing the possibilities and figuring the odds for success and failure. "This is another battle for us, but it's not the war. If we lose, we got another chance to-morrow night. So be careful; if you get a good shot at him, you take it, but you stay out of his way, and make sure you come out in one piece. In the third fall the Mask gets him in the sleeper, and you put him out. You put him out so good he don't wake up for a while."

The bell called them to the ring, and they went out

to meet the Angel, the Mask and the Claw walking bravely, the Baron and Panzer, still sore and ailing from their meeting the night before, following lamely behind. Claudius brought up the rear, and Squint stopped at the edge of the porch and watched them go. The crowd parted before them, giving them passage, and every few steps an arm reached out to touch one of the wrestlers' shoulders in sympathy.

Durwood Henry called it exactly right for the folks at home when he compared the procession to the Christians and the lions and to David and Goliath in reverse.

Squint would have told them just to wrestle fair, not to try to cheat the Angel or hurt him. But then he had talked to the Angel, to Arthur, and they hadn't, and he hadn't been able to explain it to them completely. What he was wrestling with was a good idea, one that Claudius hadn't thought of yet and one that Squint himself wouldn't work out completely until that night's exhibition was over.

37: The Depths of Despair

"This crowd tonight is not calling for the Angel's health and happiness," Durwood Henry observed. "It's calling for his blood." Almost the same time as Durwood spoke, five rows up in the stands on the far side, a hard-faced grandma with an arm like a slingshot whipped a peanut at the Angel and zinged it so close to his ear it must have sounded like a hummingbird. "One thing's for certain, ladies and gentlemen and you kids listening at home, there's gonna be some blood spilled here tonight. The only question is whose, the Angel's or the two young wrestlers' now climbing in the ring?"

The sheriff called the three wrestlers together and gave them the rules: no pulling hair, no choking, no gouging in the eyes with the fingers, no hitting with the closed fists or elbows, no scratching, no kicking below the belt. Only two wrestlers in the ring at one time for the first two falls, then by special arrangement, two against one for the third and final fall. Fifteen-minute time limit for the first two, no time limit for the third.

Then the sheriff checked the Claw's scabbard to make sure the sharp point of the hook was covered securely. The Mask went to his corner, climbed through the ropes, and watched as the Claw and the Angel squared off and waited for the bell.

Claudius kept time on the "official" stopwatch while the Baron stood ready at the side of the ring; on signal from Claudius the Baron whopped the bell with a tack hammer, and the match got going. The crowd offered the Claw encouragements and instructions, yelling things like "Rip out his gizzard!" and "Puncture his head!" Nothing like that was going to happen, of course; what was gonna happen was what wrestlers call friendly tussling. The Claw was faster on his feet and spent the first few minutes staying out of trouble. The Angel kept stalking the Claw around the ring, trapping him twice and getting him in a torture hold, not really causing great pain and not being able to keep the hold very long. There is a wrestling rule that states, "When wrestler A is maintaining a legal hold on wrestler B, and wrestler B touches any rope, wrestler A must release the hold." The rule is designed to give the wrestler Bs in the world a small chance against impossible odds, and indeed, without it there might not be any wrestler Bs left.

Squint could tell the wrestlers were stalling around, and after the third time the Claw grabbed the ropes to make Sheriff Jernigen make the Angel quit twisting his arm or head, the crowd could tell, too. Their hero wasn't acting heroic enough, and they were just about to start throwing things.

The Angel caught the Claw again in an armlock, pulled him up close, and whispered in his ear, "When I let you go, I will hit you in the head. You pretend to be hurt, then hit me and get me in a hold or two." The Angel had been around long enough to know the

Claw had to do something to make the fight interesting, or word would get around. "On three," the Angel said, and began counting.

At the count of three he relaxed his grip on the Claw's good arm, and the Claw sprang free. He wasn't free for more than a second, however, before the Angel popped him in the forehead with his open hand and sank him weakly to his knees. In a real battle the match would be ended, but in this one the Angel gave the Claw time to recover by strutting around the ring, playing the crowd as the villain. By the time he got back to the Claw, the Claw was ready. The crowd began to go wild when the Claw shot out his good hand to the side of the Angel's head, staggering the big man. The Claw managed to get his hook under one of the Angel's legs and trip him to the mat. As the Angel had promised, he let the Claw get him in a hold, in this case a leglock on the Angel's head, and keep it for a while.

The action continued until there were three and a half minutes to go in the fall; then the Claw started getting tired and tried to tag the Mask to come in and relieve him. That became the focus of the match, then, the Claw trying to reach his partner and the Angel keeping him from it. The Claw faked left and right like a halfback and would have made it around the Angel except for the hook. The Angel grabbed the hook and slung the Claw against the ropes on the opposite side of the ring. The crowd gasped in unison when they saw what had happened; the Angel was holding the scabbard in his hand; the Claw was holding up a gleaming deadly weapon.

Someone in the crowd yelled, "Stick 'im!" and someone else yelled, "Disconnect his innards!"

Durwood Henry was scared there might be a killing done. "The Claw just wants to make a tag on his partner. If I were the Angel right now, I think I'd let him make it."

The Masked Marvel was standing on the bottom ropes, holding onto the corner post and leaning as far out into the ring as his arms would let him, like trying to rescue a man drowning in quicksand or slime. The Claw advanced deliberately toward the Angel standing between him and the Mask's outstretched arm. He took a warning swipe with the hook to move the Angel out of the way, but the Angel had no intention of moving. Quick as a cobra he caught the Claw by the good hand and started swinging him around in circles like a big bullyboy playing crack-the-whip with his little sister.

Now undoubtedly the Mask could have made the tag. The reason he didn't was that he'd have to stick his hand out, or in this case *leave* his hand out, in front of that hook coming by at fifty miles an hour.

He'd put his hand out like he wanted to make the tag, but every time the sharp point of the hook came around, he lost courage and pulled it back. And that's the way the first fall ended, with the Angel finally slowing the Claw down and letting him go. The poor Claw was so dizzy he couldn't even walk to the Mask's corner. It was one step in the right direction and three in the wrong one. Just as the bell rang, he lost his balance completely and almost fell through the ropes into the screaming crowd. He would have, too, except his hook caught on the top rope as he was falling through, and he ended up tangled like a fly in a web.

A fifteen-minute intermission was announced, and everybody except Squint and those working the concession stand went in the house for R and R, which, according to Claudius, is refueling and replanning. For the refueling part, he gave the Claw two shots of strong green whiskey to steady his hands, and the Mask two shots to steady his nerves.

Squint's job was to keep the crowd entertained with Seymour. There hadn't been any gunfire for a while, so Seymour was thinking the hunters were gone and the nightmare was over, and it was easy for Squint to coax him from under the porch with a pan of raw hamburger meat and a bowl of cold beer. Seymour was grateful and ate the meat and guzzled the beer and tried to tell Squint about gunshots and what they did to his nervous system. Squint listened but couldn't do anything about it. He slipped the chain over the bear's head and led him out into the arena, there to lick fingers and catch peanuts.

Seymour and Squint worked the crowd. Seymour was almost back to being his old self again when he heard something or thought he heard something. He cocked his head up like a prairie dog listening for a hawk. The little kid, Bubba, who Seymour had carefully avoided the first night, came up and tried to lasso that head perched so intently in the night air. Seymour easily ducked the rope and then, sure that he heard what he was listening for, took off on a run for the front gate pulling the chain-holding Squint behind him.

It was a motorcycle. More specifically it was the motorcycle of McKay Brothers, and nothing sounded better on a day when people were shooting off firearms over Seymour's head than the sound of his old friend's motorcycle. Squint's arm might have been pulled off his shoulder if he hadn't been light on his feet.

Claudius was pacing the floor, feeling the time before his two wrestlers had to go back out again. "Okay," he said, "Squint says the Angel's having a change of heart; the Claw says he's a gentleman of the old school, someone who knows what he's doing, and I say he's an animal. So where does that leave us?"

"I didn't say he was a gentleman," the Claw objected; he was staring at the big clock that looked like a wristwatch on a chain. "I just said he didn't hurt me when he had a chance."

Outside in the arena, the bell clanged again.

"So what do we do? Do we got out there and fall in love, or do we got out and fight?" The fact was Claudius's plans hadn't been working out too well lately, and that tended to make a person cautious.

"I'll try to get him in the sleeper," the Mask said, and that seemed to settle the strategy.

The bell called them to the ring, and they filed out of the living room. They were on their way to the ring when Julie came through the living room from the back part of the house. She was dressed again, as she had been the first night, in her nurse's uniform—little Red Cross insignia on the shoulders of her blouse and on the pockets of her skirt. Instead of going to the nurse's table, though, she followed them down to ringside and found a place to stand in the aisle. Nobody noticed her being out of place or how she walked on her right leg like it wasn't a human leg at all but carved out of a crooked tree limb.

The Mask and the Claw climbed in the ring, and the crowd took up their hooting for blood. Mommas, poppas, grandmammas, and grandpoppas. Someone who wasn't familiar with wrestlers would have thought them insane.

Outside, when they got to the gate, Squint let the bear go; the motorcycle was coming up the road toward them, and bears, when they get excited, can run faster than thirty miles an hour.

Seymour covered the distance from the arena to the motorcycle coming across the field in no time at all. Brothers, luckily, saw him coming and veered his motorcycle and sidecar to the right at the last second, or there would've been bear hide and motorcycle parts a-flying. Seymour went straight down the road, over-running his mark, then circling, and coming back to make a running, headfirst dive into the sidecar. There was a thump, but Seymour came up smiling, and when they got up to where Squint was waiting, the bear was licking Brothers's face and goggles.

It was almost too embarrassing to look at, an animal so happy to see a human being; it almost looked like they were related. Brothers cut off the engine and had to push the bear away. "Damn bear's gone crazy," he said. Seymour began trying to tell him about the crazy things that had been going on lately, about getting kicked in the nose, about having to wear red and white checkered wrestling suits, about Bubba trying to catch his head in ropes, and about people shooting off guns. A lot had happened to the bear since he'd come to learn wrestling.

"Just settle down," Brothers told him. "If you're ready to go back to Dallas, I'll take you with me." Then he said hello to Squint, remarked how things weren't going too well. The sidecar had a radio, and Brothers had listened to the first fall on the way.

"We're gonna lose," Squint told him, not so much because he was afraid of it happening. More as a matter of fact.

When they walked into the arena, the bell had rung and the second fall was under way. The action in the ring was slow, but it wasn't because the Mask wasn't trying. The only trouble for the crowd was they didn't know what he was trying; he kept hitting the Angel in the shoulder with his arm like a bully trying to pick a fight. He was trying to get the sleeper hold on the Angel, but there were only a few people in the world who knew what he was trying to do. As far as the Angel was concerned, it was a bully trying to pick a fight. The crowd clapped and cheered at how brave the Mask was, antagonizing the monster like that. All Squint could do was close his eyes.

Four or five minutes must have gone by with the Angel grabbing the Mask in a loose hold and letting the Mask break it, only to have the Mask step back and hit him in the shoulder again. If the crowd was starting to get a bit confused, so was the Angel.

"What in the Sam Hill you trying to do?" the Angel finally had to ask, whispering, not asking out loud where people at ringside could hear him. Of course, there was no way the Mask could tell him; you don't tell your opponent what you're trying to do. When the Mask didn't answer and when he didn't try anything else, or cooperate, that's when the Angel started getting mad. The first thing he did was give a low growl, like a family dog, to warn you that if you come a step farther or look at him cross-eyed, there is going to be hair flying in the breeze. Everybody in the arena could see what was about to happen, and there wasn't anybody in the Mask's place who wouldn't have backed off.

What happened then happened almost too fast for words. The Angel grabbed the Mask with both of his massive hands locked together behind the Mask's back in a crusher hold.

"Whatever you do, stay out of his way," Claudius had warned, but the warning didn't matter much now.

Like the first fight, the second one would've been history, except at that point Julie reached under her skirt and pulled out the pearl-handled pistol she'd taken from Ranger Ralph's holster and tied to her right leg, which had made her walk funny. The pistol in hand, she pointed it right at the Angel's head, aiming to shoot him right between his two alligator-looking eyes, and pulled the trigger.

The only trouble was the bullets in Ranger Ralph's pistol were blanks. The wad of cotton from the blank cartridge hit the Angel right where Julie was aiming, and the Angel must have thought it was the end. The shot was perfectly placed, over the Mask's shoulder and close by his ear; if the cotton wad had touched either the Mask's shoulder or ear, the Mask would have thought he'd been killed; as it was, it was a pure Annie Oakley shot, and the Angel fainted dead away, crumpling at the Mask's feet.

After the sound of the pistol cleared the air, there wasn't any air, it seemed. Everybody in the crowd was suddenly quiet, thinking that after all these years of hoping to see, even dreaming about seeing, somebody actually kill somebody else, they'd finally seen it. The Angel of Sorrow was lying motionless and quiet in the middle of the ring.

The only thing missing was blood. There wasn't any blood anywhere, and that caused Claudius to crawl into the ring partway and prod the Angel with his finger. Julie's hand went limp with second thoughts about what she'd done, and the Ranger's pistol dropped in the dirt. The woman in the crowd who'd whipped the peanut so close to the Angel's ear earlier now took out her handkerchief, sniffled, and blew her nose. Claudius poked the Angel again, and the Angel moaned.

"Hell," Claudius said, "he ain't dead. He just got scared so bad he went to sleep."

The Angel moved his arm a little and, after a moment or two of waking up and feeling himself with his hands to see if he was really dead or not, started to sit up. The crowd was relieved some, and the sheriff, who could see the headlines, "SHERIFF BURL JERNIGEN OFFICIATES AT KILLING" and "SHERIFF BURL JERNIGEN LOSES ELECTION BY LANDSLIDE," was also relieved.

Everybody was relieved except Claudius, who was already thinking of what to do next and crawling under the ropes. He jumped down in the aisle, took the hammer from the Baron's hand, and rang the bell to end the round. "Don't just stand there," he yelled at the sheriff. "Give us the round."

The Angel was getting up from the mat, but by then it was all over; the sheriff was raising the Mask's hand, awarding him the round.

Squint was weak in the knees, but Brothers acted like he'd seen that kind of act a million times before and was even laughing. "That damned Claudius," he said, appreciating the quality of the act he'd just seen. "There ain't a better hard-knocking, double-scheming businessman anywhere, is there, Seymour?"

They looked around for Seymour, but the bear had made tracks for a friendlier environment. If Squint and Brothers had looked outside, they'd have seen him in the moonlight, disappearing over the distant hill rise, running like the gates of Bear Heaven had been swung open in front of him but were slowly swinging closed, and the fires of Bear Hell were licking at his backside.

"Can't tell it too much now," Brothers sadly observed, "but that old bear used to be quite a trouper."

Claudius was on the loudspeaker then, calming the crowd down and announcing the last intermission of the evening.

38: The Death of the Masked Marvel, the Untimely End of the Steel Claw

Now nobody knows for sure what Karp told the Angel to get him ready for the final fall; as always, they'd gone back to the trailer and locked the doors. Whatever he told him, however, had its effect.

They came together in the center of the ring, all three of them, only one had blood in his eye, and the other two had faraway looks. The Angel of Sorrow was ready to get serious with them. They were ready to leave for China, or Afghanistan, or someplace where wrestling had never been heard of and the Angel of Sorrow was somebody fictitious, like the bogeyman that parents used to scare their heathen children. The Angel never really gave them a chance.

With his superhuman strength, he could have snapped the Mask's arms like dry twigs in the Great American Desert; instead, he only bent them useless while he kept the Claw at bay with bone-jarring kicks to the chest. The Angel fought like an Alaskan husky, first crippling one wing of one opponent, then leaving him to lick his wounds while he crippled the other.

Brothers and Squint were at ringside with Claudius and the others to witness the executions, groaning and shouting encouragement, but mostly groaning. "Them boys ain't got a chance," Brothers dryly pointed out to anybody who didn't realize it for himself. "If they was smart, they'd roll over and play possum."

Poor Julie was hiding her eyes, refusing to watch the massacre. Her ears told her everything she wanted to know.

The Angel went after the Claw, and it should be pointed out that the Claw's hook was protected once again by the little leather scabbard. The Claw, thus without a weapon, was backpedaling around the ring, trying to stay out of the Angel's way till the Mask could shake off his injuries and get back in the fight.

It didn't work, of course. The Angel caught him in one of the corners and held onto the hook arm with one hand and ripped off the scabbard with the other. That puzzled a few people, the Claw included, until they saw what the Angel's intention was. Using his huge strength, he forced the Claw's arm to one of the turnbuckles that held up the ropes, stuck the hook through it, and began bending the steel. It didn't take much more than twenty seconds for the Angel to bend the steel hook round like a pretzel. Just about the time that the Mask had recovered, the Claw was hopelessly trapped. Claudius took off for the house to get the hacksaw, and when he came running back with it, the Claw saw it and started screaming, "No! No! No!" Nothing the Angel had done hurt him as much as what Claudius did, and that was to saw off his hook.

The Angel, in the meantime, was back after the Mask and had him captured in the corner. He grabbed the younger, smaller wrestler by his most vulnerable part, his mask, and started jerking his head back and forth like a demented baboon trying to tear the skin off a football. He got a finger in each of the earholes and pulled, and the mask started ripping. The Mask had both hands, still weak from the awful wrenching they'd suffered before, on the mask, trying to hold it together, but with little use. A large hunk came out on the right side; then an even larger hunk came out of the left. The mask was kind of lying across the top of the Mask's head like a damp towel, and the Mask was holding it down front and back. The Angel stuck his finger in the mouth hole, luckily on the outside of the Mask's own lips, and ripped downward. Another rip in the back, and the Mask was standing in the corner with nothing but the purple circles that circled his eyes, whimpering like a little kid who's lost his favorite teddy bear to burglars.

And that's the way the fight ended, not with the mighty bang of breaking bones, but with the whimper of lost pride. When the Angel pinned the Mask's shoulders to the mat, the Mask could hardly resist, holding the purple circles over his eyes to protect his identity as he was. And by that time Claudius had sawed through the hook and the Claw was free. Claudius was telling him to get in there and save the Mask, but the Claw was in a state of shock. There wasn't anything the sheriff could do but end the match and lift the Angel of Sorrow's arm.

It was a sad night all around. There wasn't any more Steel Claw, because there wasn't any claw, and there wasn't any Masked Marvel, because there wasn't any mask. They gave the Mask a pillowcase to wear over his head so he could have use of his hands and not have to hold those little circles up all night. The only thing they could do for the Claw was to offer him sympathy and try not to look at the stub.

They had lost the match, and Seymour had run off. But Seymour would come back because there just wasn't any place for a bear to go in Texas, and they were sure to win the next night's match because Squint had come up with his plan.

PART THREE

39: Things Take a Turn for the Better

In defeat the seeds of victory are sown, Claudius told himself. The words sounded nice in his mind, like something somebody important must have said one time, Henry IV, or Richard III, or one of the Presidents or somebody. If nobody important had said it, however, he was willing to take credit for it himself.

His bedroom was at the back of the house, the opposite end of the upstairs hall from Squint's. It was the bedroom that had been his and Constance's back in the old days. From the window he could see his old thinking chair starting to warm up in the morning sun. How much thinking and scheming had he done in that chair over the years? he wondered. How many times had that chair saved his life by getting him away from Constance's mean-talking tongue? Now it seemed to him that he didn't need the chair so much, and might ought to haul it back down to the basement or give it to Squint. A thinking man could do his thinking anywhere.

He'd slept better in that old bed than he'd ever slept before and had had one of his better dreams. In his dream he was traveling with that all-girl troupe of softball players, and he was propped up on cushions on the wide back seat of the bus. The bus was parked beside a peaceful river; it was twilight, and soft music was coming from somewhere. He had a beer in one hand and a glass of champagne in the other, and when he wasn't taking a sip of one or the other, one of those women would stick something delicious in his mouth to eat. They had a turkey leg and some Gulf shrimp dipped in tartar sauce and a barbecue sandwich that was so good it had to be flown in from Memphis. That seemed like it went on for hours, and while the women weren't the best-looking women in the world, they were more than kind. The only bad part about the dream was the part just before he woke up. Glenda, the team's big catcher, had pulled off his boots and socks and was soaking his feet in warm rose water, and he had the distinct feeling that they were planning to use him in some kind of human sacrifice. "Ain't he the sweetest, best-hearted man in the world?" they kept saying. He woke up without ever knowing what they were planning to do, but whatever it was he had been perfectly willing to let them do it.

Because he *was* sweet and he *was* bighearted. He had to be to do what he was about to do that night. The others in the house didn't know about it yet, but they'd know about it soon.

When he came downstairs, he found Julie and the Mask in the kitchen, Julie cooking bacon and eggs and the Mask, his head still in the pillowcase, sitting at the table looking at pictures in a wrestling catalog.

"Look at this one," he said to Claudius, and held up the catalog open to a picture of a man wearing a white mask that covered his head, with red and gold flames that seemed to burn out of the eyes, around the side-burns, and up the back of the head. "This is the Captain America model, and this one . . ." He turned the page to another picture, one of a stout young man in a threatening pose wearing a bright blue bird cowl with a real-looking hawk's beak over the nose. "This is the Hawk, or this one I kinda like . . ." The third picture was called the Mysterious Mister X, and the mask was scarlet and fierce with inch-wide strips of green satin making the letter X across the face. "Julie likes the Hawk the best because it lets my chin and mouth out."

"I like the Hawk, I think," Claudius said, agreeing with his daughter that the chin was better than nothing.

The Mask considered it. "When a hawk ain't fighting or hunting, you're supposed to keep his head covered with a sack, aren't you?" It seemed he'd seen that one time in a movie; this outlaw leader had this fighting hawk and kept a little black tobacco sack over its head. While he was waiting for his Hawk mask to come in, it would be all right to wear the pillowcase; it wouldn't be unmanly or anything.

"The Hawk it is," the Mask announced. While he ate breakfast, he filled out the order form, licking the stub of the pencil and checking back and forth between the picture numbers and the order form. One mistake, and he'd get the wrong mask and end up being Alligator Man, with green scales and warts all over his head, or Mad Modred, with a head like a ripe cantaloupe.

The Claw came in while the Mask and Julie were eating. Claudius was still stuffed from his dream and was taking only coffee and a morning cigar. "All that's great for you," the Claw told the Mask, "but what am

I going to do about *this?*" The Claw had a wool sock over the stub of what used to be his hook; he showed it to them, and they looked at it sadly. "There ain't nothing in that catalog for me." It was a catalog for masks only, not for claws.

"We'll get you something," Claudius said. "I think I saw a real claw, one of them mechanical hands like the Army wanted to give you in the first place, at a medical supply store in Dallas."

"Aw, those things are ugly," the Claw said. "They look like lobster pinchers."

Claudius thought about it. "How 'bout we take it over to Neiman-Marcus and have it gold-plated? Then, instead of the Steel Claw, we call you the Golden Claw. Make for a great team, won't it, the Hawk and the Golden Claw."

The idea of a gold claw and a new name pleased the Claw so much he didn't care what the thing looked like. It could look like a turtle head, and it wouldn't matter. If he got it, he'd keep it shiny and new-looking all his life.

The Mask and Julie left to put the order for his new mask in the mailbox and bring back the morning paper.

The Baron and Panzer were up then, as were Betty and Rose and Herman. "Good news," the Baron said, taking his arm out of the sling and flexing his muscle.

"I think my arm's healed up nicely."

"And I think my leg's okay," Panzer announced, putting his crutches aside and hitting himself in the thigh with his fist.

Ranger Ralph and Hog Jarvis had spent the night and were planning to leave after breakfast, so Herman was again cooking for more than a half dozen people, which meant more than two dozen eggs. No skillet was big enough, so he ended up scrambling them in the turkey roaster.

"No," Claudius told Panzer and the Baron, "I want you boys to keep your ailments one more day. Keep the sling and crutches going at least till tomorrow."

The two wrestlers were mystified by what Claudius was asking them to do, but they didn't stay mystified long. The Mask and Julie came running in with the morning paper, and there on the front page of the sports section was the picture of Claudius from the mantel, the one of him and his medal and frock coat. The headline was in the boldest letters the Tyler newspaper could find, and they hadn't been used since the war ended. "GAINS TO WRESTLE ANGEL," it said.

It was Ranger Ralph who made the first comment.. "I feel sorry for the undertaker who's gonna have to work on your mangled corpse. He just may have to bury you in a knot." The others were in complete agreement, including the Hog, who was going "Snorka-

snorka-gomp-gomp-gomp," but Claudius had been expecting some kind of lack of confidence on their parts. He just looked at the end of his cigar for a few seconds; then he got up and walked to the screen door. A pretty red cardinal was whistling on the wire by the porch, and Claudius spent a minute or two whistling back, practicing his birdcalls.

"The Angel's tough, all right," Claudius finally said, "but I reckon me and my partner can handle him." He walked over to big Herman, put his arm around him, and smiled.

40: An Errand of Great Importance

With all the excitement Claudius's announcement made, it was almost noon before anybody noticed that Squint and McKay Brothers were gone. Claudius told them that the two had left early on the motorcycle for Dallas on a matter of great importance, and if they didn't dally, they'd be back before the fight.

Even as he spoke, however, Brothers was easing the motorcycle off the paved highway into the gravel parking lot of a hamburger joint, known from its only sign as Eat. He turned off the engine, took off his goggles, and took a hard pull from the flask. "I can't pass this place without gitting one of their cheeseburgers," he said, but Squint couldn't hear him. The trouble with motorcycles was you couldn't talk while you were riding on them, and you couldn't hear after you got off.

You couldn't walk too well either. Squint almost tripped on the rickety steps on the way in. About the only one of his senses that wasn't still vibrating from the ride was his sense of smell; Brothers saw him sniffing the air of the café and laughed. "You know the cheeseburgers gotta be good because the place smells like a cheeseburger." Mounted on the hood over the grill where you had to look at it was a framed and official-looking picture of General Eisenhower. Old Ike smiled at you the whole time you ate.

Outside, a home-painted car, with so many different fenders and parts from other cars on it you couldn't tell what the original make was, pulled into the lot, and four barefooted farm boys got out. McKay Brothers watched them get out and point at the motorcycle and sidecar and start making fun of it, one of them standing up in the sidecar and another one playing zoom-zoom with the handlebars. Squint was afraid they'd do something to hurt it, and too much depended on their getting to Dallas and back. He was worried about stopping for cheeseburgers in the first place; now he was even more worried. Brothers, on the other hand, was as calm as a mud hen in a back-

yard pond. He just walked over to the door and yelled,
"You boys get away from that machinery and come up
here; I want to give you something." He took his
wallet out of his pocket, and they must have thought
he was gonna give them money. Instead, he gave them
each a card, saying, "These cards are good any time
of the year, and it ain't that far over to Dallas, so come
and see me sometimes. This card will get you in free,
and you'll get to ride the Caterpillar, and the Octopus, and the Wild Mouse. Any of you boys ever get to
ride the Wild Mouse?"

The answer from all four was: "Heck, no."

"Well, you'll come see me, and I'll put you on that
thing and give you something to talk about."

Thus Brothers turned a potentially dangerous situation into a friendly one. The four boys crawled in a
booth, looked at their cards, and ordered double
cheeseburgers.

Squint was impressed, but Brothers didn't even con-
sider it an accomplishment. "You want to see somebody handle rubes, you should've seen Claudius when
he was with the circus. I'll swear, he had the power to
cloud men's minds; once there was a man with a
hatchet after him, fully intending to carve up his head.
Somebody in the circus had told the man Claudius was
a Yankee, a communist, and about to run off with his
wife. All of it was a joke—Claudius hadn't ever seen

212 ON THE ROPES

the man before in his life. Anyway, Claudius got out of it by guessing the man's name. Thigpen. He'd raised the hatchet up to take a swipe at Claudius's head, and your daddy just looked at him and said, 'Hold it right there, Thigpen; you can't kill me 'cause I'm your cousin.' "

"How can you guess a name like Thigpen?" Squint wanted to know, but there wasn't any answer.

"He just had the instincts," was all Brothers could say, but he looked at Squint and considered the boy. "You ought to know what instincts are; I've noticed you've got them, too."

All of Squint's instincts were telling him that it was time to get back on the road again. He didn't say it; all he had to do was think it, and Brothers knew what he was thinking.

"Okay," Brothers said, paying the bill at the counter, "let's go try it again."

Just as he was about to pull back on the highway, he stopped and took out the flask. He would have taken another snort, but Squint stopped him with his eyes. "Yeah, you got it all right," Brothers said. He gave the flask reluctantly to Squint for safekeeping and told him, "Don't give me any more of it till we get right here on the way back."

41: A Lost Soul Returns

Time might pass quickly when you're having fun, but it drags out forever when you're just waiting. The wrestlers, Julie, and Herman were all having a terrible day in terms of time passing slowly. After they'd been told what was going to happen that night and had had their parts in it explained, for them, there was mostly just waiting. Betty and Rose were the only ones with something to do, and all they were doing was sizing up material that might be used for Herman's and Claudius's costumes. Claudius was the only one happy, whistling and showing off on the pool table.

In a way, it was strange and sad that it was all ending, the three nights of championship wrestling and the whole two weeks of racing against the bank. They'd been so busy for so long, getting the house ready, building the arena, working to get everything ready and keep things going right, that there hadn't been one argument among the ten of them, or the eleven and twelve of them, if you counted Seymour and Brothers. That alone would have been considered miraculous, but they had to add to that the fact that two of them had even fallen in love, and it probably wouldn't be long before a whole new crop of wrestlers would be in the making. That night, one way or another, it was going to end.

"You people are looking like hungry buzzards just ate your roses," Claudius told them, careening the cue ball around five rails before watching it strike the eight ball, nudging it into the side pocket. "If you feel like being sorry for anybody, try feeling sorry for the Angel of Sorrow. Just think, he's never lost a wrestling match in his whole life, just like I was on this table before that slicker beat me, and tonight the Angel's gonna lose his first fight. Now that's something to feel sad about, not being able to stand up and say, 'I've never been beat.' "

They should have been cheered up with that, but somehow, they weren't, and the afternoon dragged on and on.

The only thing that happened to break the monotony of waiting was the return of Seymour. The poor creature came in the back door, whimpering like a lonesome puppy that had just endured a spring thunderstorm in an open city doorway, and indeed, he had been out all night, and indeed, there had been thunderstorms a few miles to the north of them. He couldn't say where he'd spent the night, but it hadn't been in a luxury hotel. His checkered wrestling outfit was covered with cockleburs and infested with barn lice.

He also had to go to the bathroom pretty bad and hadn't been able to with nobody to undo his flaps for him in back.

"Take them britches off that critter this instant,"

Betty instructed. "I think they're the perfect size for Herman."

42: Eats Live Chickens

The McKay Brothers Good Times Amusement Park was one of those vanishing species of big-city amusement parks time was passing by. Its main feature over the years had been the main auditorium, a tremendous gray wood and plaster structure that could seat almost five thousand people around a stage big enough for elephants and high-wire acts. Around the building there were smaller structures built on, lean-tos that housed the permanent sideshows—the Tunnel of Love, the Cascade of Horrors, the Penny Arcade with the whirling girlie peep shows, mechanical steam shovel machines, and others. Facing the stalls and forming a midway were the rides—the Caterpillar, the Octopus, and the Wild Mouse that Brothers had mentioned, a Ferris Wheel, a Skyride, and a few others. Between the rides were the ticket booths and the tent stalls where they told fortunes, sold cotton candy and pennants, had the games where people tried to knock down the milk bottles, bust the balloons with darts, or pick the right floating duck with the lucky number on the bottom.

Squint's only visit to Dallas had been the week be-

fore, when he'd come to find Claudius, and that had
been his first time in any big city, so naturally he was
still impressed with the sights. The thing that impressed him most about the Good Times Amusement
Park was the idea that a fair could be a permanent
thing. When the fair came to Tyler, it didn't stay but
a week, and he'd never gotten to stay more than a few
hours of one measly day. Brothers drove the motorcycle down the midway from one end to the other,
and Squint was thinking how lucky the kids in Dallas
were to have such a thing. The motorcycle stopped at
the last tent, the one that had the freak shows, the Fat
Lady and the Geek, with their pictures on banners in
front. The Geek's picture showed a wild-looking white-
haired man with a chicken head in his mouth and
blood running down his chin, and it had across the
bottom, "EATS LIVE CHICKENS."

Squint had to know. "Does he really eat live chickens?"

"Course he does," Brothers told him, looking at the
boy with reproach. "Do you think I'd have an act that
wasn't honest?"

It was the live chicken eater that Brothers had
stopped to talk to. "He used to be a dentist before he
looked down one mouth too many; something snapped
in his brain, and now, you know, he kinda likes eating
chickens. Now whatever you do, don't mention mouths

or teeth, and don't stare at his mouth or he'll run away again, and it ain't easy to find anybody who'll do what he does."

It was the Geek who knew where everything was in the old storage barn, and what they were there to get from the barn, only the Geek could find.

They walked through the tent and through the open back flap that let them out and into a small courtyard formed by three old circus trailers. In front of one of the trailers was a chicken coop full of nervous hens, and standing near the coop at a setup card table, boiling an egg in a pan of water on a hot plate, was the Geek. White-haired and old, he looked exactly like the picture in front, except a bit wilder, like he knew the secret of the universe and nobody would believe him.

"Frank," Brothers introduced him, "this is Squint Gains, Claudius's kid."

"Claudius's kid," the Geek repeated, narrowing his eyes and giving Squint a visual searching. "You want to see me do it, don't you?"

Squint knew exactly what he was talking about, and so did the chickens because when he snapped his head around and looked at them, they all started clucking in terror and tried to hide behind each other. Squint was pretty sure he didn't want to see it, but he didn't know how to say so.

"We ain't got time for that." Brothers saved him. "We're just here to pick up that cylinder of gunk we used to use in the clown act. You know where it is?"

The word "cylinder" reminded the Geek of something he didn't want to be reminded of—oxygen came in cylinders, laughing gas came in cylinders. A glazed look came in his eyes, but he didn't go crazy. Instead, he calmly went to the coop and grabbed up one of the terrified chickens. Squint was afraid to watch, but the hen went calm in the Geek's hands, like it was numb or resigned to its fate, and the Geek started petting its head and neck. He wasn't going to bite the head off, at least not immediately, and Squint opened his eyes. "I'll show you where it is," the Geek said, petting the chicken like a little kid pets his favorite blanket, hugging it up to the side of his face.

Squint and Brothers followed with the motorcycle behind the Geek and the chicken as he walked to the storage barn. Squint didn't go in, and it was probably a good thing he didn't as he had inherited Claudius's squeamishness for real blood and tended to faint at the sight of it. Even sitting in the sidecar outside the building, he knew that Brothers and the Geek had found the cylinder. The sight of it must have been too much for Frank because Squint heard Brothers shout, "NO! Don't!" And he heard the chicken.

Squint made up his mind then and there that no

matter whatever else he did in life, and it didn't matter what he did, he'd never be a dentist.

43: Fourteen Voices Raised in Song

On toward late afternoon another catastrophe was avoided, or as Claudius would have put it, the specter of adversity came sniffing around the bacon. It came in the person of Deacon Lawrence Rambo, who arrived with Sheriff Burl Jernigen, the siren on top of Burl's automobile blazing away. Burl liked to have that siren going, especially in the election season, because it let people know for miles around that their sheriff was on the job. Sometimes at night he would turn it on and pretend he was chasing somebody out of the county just so people could sleep more soundly in their beds. He couldn't do that too often, however, because it made it seem like too many of his customers were getting away. This time it was for official business; an official paper had to be delivered.

Everybody in the house came to the front gate of the arena to see what the siren was for, and Burl stated the nature of his call. "This here is a petition of sixty-eight names asking you to cease and desist professional wrestling on these premises immediately and permanently or suffer the consequences."

Deacon Rambo stood beside the sheriff, the deacon's eyes smoldering in the glory that comes from doing his Maker's work; he meant for his gaze to melt his opponents to their knees, but Claudius stepped up and met him dagger for dagger. Nobody was going to give the bad eye to Claudius without getting it right back.

"I'd like to see the names on that petition," Claudius said, gently taking the piece of paper from the sheriff's hand. He glanced over the names, Mrs. Thelma Hinds, Mrs. Alice Harrell, Mrs. Ramona Lynn Peacock, Miss Matilda Ross Jenkins. . . . The first fourteen names were all members of the Good News Choir and Men's Auxiliary Quartet; the rest of the names he recognized as belonging to the deacon's flock. He smiled and asked Rambo, "You want to tell me what the consequences are?"

Burl, acting like a kind of interpreter as the deacon was refusing to talk to Claudius, turned officially to Rambo. "Mr. Gains says he wants to know what the consequences are."

"You can tell Mr. Gains that I intend to lay my body down in the road, to forfeit my very life if that's necessary, to keep the good people of this county out of the clutches of this infidel." The deacon delivered his ultimatum, his face white and his soft hands shaking.

It was all Claudius could do to keep from laughing. He had been wondering what he was going to do for a preliminary act, and here one had been delivered to him. "Uh, let me think about this a minute and see if I can't think of a better way." Everyone waited in silence as Claudius did his thinking; then he handed the petition back to the sheriff, and it was so much for the better way. "We'll take the consequences," he announced.

Sheriff Jernigen was afraid Claudius was going to say that. "Claudius," he grieved, "that means I ain't gonna be able to referee tonight; I mean, if this fool really lays down in front of one of them vehicles, you know . . . the election coming up and all."

That too fitted right into Claudius's plans. For dramatic effect he was going to announce that he and Herman were wrestling the Angel "no holds barred— no time limit and getting-saved-by-the-bell—no referee in the ring." There was nothing people liked better than a no-holds-barred massacre.

He wished the sheriff and the deacon good luck in their separate undertakings and excused himself to do some quick telephoning.

In the hall by the phone, he momentarily felt sorry for the deacon for having come so far along in life without understanding the first thing about real people. The names he started looking up in the telephone book were Mrs. Thelma Hinds, Mrs. Alice Harrell, Mrs. Ramona Lynn Peacock, Miss Matilda Ross Jenkins, and ten others.

For his preliminary act, in respect for what the

deacon was going to do out front, Claudius was going to present a spiritual concert, fourteen lovely voices raised in song.

44: The Long Road Home

With their business in Dallas done, for Squint and Brothers it was time to knuckle down to some hard highway driving. The road home is always longer than the road away from home, even when it's the same road and you've measured it a thousand times. The café called Eat was outside the town of Mineola, almost exactly halfway between Tyler and Dallas, and since it had taken them two hours on the motorcycle to get there the first time, common sense said it wouldn't take but two hours to get from there back. But it would seem like more.

Squint was against stopping, but Brothers insisted on it. He also insisted on having his flask of whiskey back, saying, "You got to eat and drink to keep from getting dizzy, my boy. And if you ever get dizzy on a motorcycle, the trucks will get you." As if to emphasize his words, a big semi hauling culverts roared past on the highway. Brothers ordered two cheeseburgers to go at the takeout window and took a nasty pull from the flask.

Squint, in the meantime, was checking out the clock

and doing some quick figuring. If the first match lasted thirty minutes and they had two ten-minute intermissions and one fifteen-minute one, that would mean Claudius and Herman would be climbing in the ring at eight-ten or eight-fifteen at the latest. It was five minutes after six as they stood waiting for the cheeseburgers to cook, and the cheeseburgers hadn't even started sizzling yet.

They might be as much as ten minutes late, which wouldn't be so bad under normal circumstances. Ten minutes wasn't important unless you were in the ring and fighting the Angel of Sorrow; then every second you stayed alive would be golden.

And there were other problems. First, after they got there, they would still have to unload the cylinder and get it up somewhere near the ring. There was a hose on top where the stuff came out, but it wasn't a very long hose, and it couldn't be aimed accurately. That created the second problem, as Squint saw it: how to get the stuff on the Angel without its looking like out-and-out cheating.

Squint had gotten his idea on how to beat the Angel the night before when he was out in front of the arena with Seymour and Brothers came in on the motorcycle. It reminded him of the week before, when Brothers had come the first time and shown them the film of Claudius getting shot out of a cannon and, before that, the film of the clowns playing baseball where stuff in buckets was thrown on them and suddenly none of them could stand up. The idea hadn't been that great; he'd simply asked Claudius if the stuff they'd thrown on the clowns to make them fall down was real, and if it was, why couldn't they use it on the Angel?

The stuff was real all right. It was called Slick-ums, and it had been invented by a mad scientist who'd tried to sell it to the Army as a new, secret weapon. And the Army would've bought it if they could've figured out who to use it on. It worked. There wasn't any doubt that it worked. If they sprayed it on the side of a hill, it would make the hill so slippery nobody could get up it, but nobody could get down it either. The Army got eight or ten cylinders to test, and the cylinders eventually ended up in a surplus store in Abilene, where Claudius bought them for the circus. The first time he'd used it, he'd used it on Brothers; he'd caught Brothers sitting on the john and sprayed his feet with it. Poor Brothers was crying and begging for somebody to help him get up. His feet didn't have any traction at all, and he couldn't hardly even get his pants up.

Brothers had been pretty sure they still had some of it in the barn in Dallas, and luckily they'd found it. Now all they had to do was get it back.

"Hell, don't worry so much," Brothers reassured

Squint; the boy's eyes were little more than slits in the front of his head, and he was watching the road like a hay farmer watches the weather rise. "We ain't gonna be more than ten minutes late, and if your daddy couldn't handle ten minutes, he'da been dead a long time ago. A few minutes ain't gonna matter."

45: The Deacon Learns About Human Nature

And as everything turned out, ten minutes didn't matter. The preliminary event, which was singing, not wrestling, was delayed by more than that by the deacon's body, which was lying in the middle of the dusty road to the arena, from which the deacon was refusing to move.

He had already caused one fistfight, between the driver of the second car in line, who wanted the deacon run over, and the driver of the first car, who was a Yankee and refused to do what was clearly his civic duty. In no time at all, ten cars, trucks, buses, and tractors were lined up behind the first and second cars. Then, down by the main road, one automobile bumped another, and a second fistfight broke out. The sheriff had his hands full, running back and forth between the deacon and the arguments that broke out here and there along the line. He'd go put out a fight; then he'd come back and talk to the deacon. "Aw, come on now, you're getting your black suit all dirty and dusty down there, and if you keep it up, I'm just gonna have to arrest you." The truth was, the sheriff was waiting for more people, which meant more voters, to show up and watch him make the proper arrest.

Now the sheriff was acting like what was going on was serious business and demanded a serious public official like himself to handle it, but deep in his heart he was tickled to death and could barely keep from laughing. The deacon was pretty happy himself, and for good reasons: First of all, he was doing what he'd said he'd do, keeping good Christian souls out of the den of iniquity, and second of all, nobody had run over him yet. It was happening just like the Good Book promised; nobody was willing to cast the first stone. "I don't care what happens to my suit or even my whole body," the deacon kept saying. "My soul is bound for glory."

Claudius and everybody else were watching from the top bleachers, leaning over the top of the billboard advertising the cure for athlete's foot. There were acres of good, dry, passable land all around the deacon, and anybody at any time could've simply gotten off the almost-nonexistent dirt road and driven up to the arena on an overland trail. The trouble was everybody who could see what was going on was watching, and everybody who couldn't see was wondering what the holdup was. "People are really like ants," Claudius observed. "They'll stay in line heads and tails till something happens to mess up the line; then they'll take off in every direction 'cept up; then, when you're not watching, they'll be back in line again, heading in the same direction."

As if to mark his words, from far under the highway there came an old Trailways bus, the destination sign above the windshield saying "The Promised Land." The bus was carrying the Good News Choir and Men's Auxiliary Quartet, and when it came upon the line of cars blocking its way, it simply pulled into the passing lane and whipped around everybody. When it got to the cutoff to the arena, it took to the ditch and came up the other side like a bulldozer, pushing a little dirt and scrubgrass out of the way, but otherwise not even slowing down.

It was Miss Matilda Ross Jenkins behind the wheel of the bus, and she had no intentions of stopping for anything. She did slow down, though, and opened the front door to see who was lying down in the road. When she saw it was the deacon and saw him sit up and wave for them to stop, she knew what he was up to and knew where her duties lay. She quickly pulled the lever to close the door and rammed her foot through the gas pedal. When the Good News Choir was invited to sing somewhere, they were going to sing, and that was all there was to it.

All of a sudden everybody was back in the cars, trucks, and buses, and instead of one new trail being broken that night, there were fifty or a hundred. You couldn't tell much because the dust was so thick you could've planted corn in it.

When it cleared, the deacon was standing up, bewildered, and the sheriff was leading him away to jail.

46: The Grand Finale, the Big Casino, the Hard Cheese, or Whatever You Want to Call It

Claudius had roped off fourteen seats just to the left of the main aisle on the way in. The choir filled those seats and sat quietly humming their warm-ups as the crowd came in. When the stands were nearly full, they broke into their first song—"Oh for a Faith That Will Not Shrink, Tho' Washed by Many a Foe" —and there were many in the crowd who'd heard them before and thought they never sounded better, and there were others who were less reverent and yelled out "Shirt!" right when the choir sang "Faith."

They sang their hearts out, happy to be singing at a joyous occasion instead of the funerals and memorial services they'd been singing at lately. They sang "Everywhere You Go, the Sunshine Follows You," "How Much Is That Doggie in the Window?" "The Happy Wanderer," which Mrs. Thelma Hinds and Mrs. Ramona Lynn Peacock yodeled, and a few more of the popular favorites. Julie came over and handed Alice Harrell the American flag, and everybody in the arena stood up at attention while Alice held the flag aloft and the choir did their concert version of "The Star-Spangled Banner," starting with "The Eyes of Texas Are Upon You," slipping into "Onward Christian Soldiers," and finally into the national anthem they were supposed to sing in the first place. They had just sung "and the home . . . of the . . . brave" when the dying strains were replaced by the sound of a motorcycle engine coming around the outside of the arena and stopping at the back door.

There's probably nothing in the world more exciting than going into a battle when everything you've got is committed on one side and everything they've got is against you on the other. The only thing Claudius could compare to the way he felt that night was D-Day, when old Ike himself came down to the barges to wish his boys good luck. It was exciting, but it was also sad because the excitement never lasted long enough, and after it was over, things returned to being boring: no more hoping, planning, or scheming.

They brought in the cylinder, and the Baron came up with the idea of painting red crosses on it and taking it down to ringside like it was emergency oxygen. Claudius had already thought of the idea of sticking carpenter's tacks through the soles of his shoes so that the points would stick in the canvas, and while they painted the crosses, Claudius hammered in the tacks.

"You know," he said, finishing the last shoe and slipping it on his foot and tying it, "nothing is going to be the same when this is over." He walked around and tested his shoes on Constance's good carpet. He walked over and looked at himself in the closet door mirror. He was wearing his Stetson hat, his frock-tailed coat with the medal on the pocket, a pair of black wool swimming trunks with "Georgia Tech" stitched over the pocket, and black silk socks held up by garters. He looked more like a hobo who had lost his pants than he did a warrior. "When this is all over, I'll be remembered as the man who beat the Angel of Sorrow. I'll probably be spending half my time signing autographs and the other half collecting money. People are gonna want me to say I wear their kind of socks, or drink their kind of beer, or spray their smelly chemicals under my arms."

That's when he got the idea on how to get the Slickums on the Angel.

Since Claudius was gonna be in the ring, Durwood Henry got the honor of acting as the master of ceremonies. He had the microphone for the loudspeaker stretched down to the ring, and he climbed in to thank the women and men of the choir for their spirited singing, and invited them to stay and watch the wrestling. That was a wasted gesture because a road grader couldn't have moved those women out of their seats.

"Ladies and gentlemen," he began, addressing the crowd, "I know it don't seem like it, but it was only a little over a week ago that Claudius Gains took this worthless hunk of farmed-out land and founded the Constance M. Gains Memorial Arena and his Famous Wrestlers' College. In that one short week he has brought to Tyler, Texas, some of the greatest entertainment we've seen around here since the days when Claudius ran the local pool hall and entertained us with his pool-shooting ability."

"Skinned us out of our money, you mean!" somebody in the crowd yelled out. Durwood just ignored the comment and went on.

"Now everybody who knows Claudius Gains knows he can do just about everything he sets his mind to, and last week he offered a prize of ten thousand dollars cash money to anybody who could beat his wrestlers. What's happened since then, ladies and gentlemen, is history. There has come amongst us a man calling himself the Angel of Sorrow, after that prize money, and he has beaten up four of Claudius Gains's top wrestlers. Not only did he beat them up good, he damn well near killed two of them. I'll tell you what it reminds me of; it reminds me of the Alamo, where eventually everybody, even the cooks and the old-timers, had to get in the fight."

In those days all you had to do to get yelling and shouting from a crowd was to play "Dixie" or mention the Alamo. They started whistling and stomping their feet and sounding like a John Wayne cattle drive. Durwood had them hypnotized by his golden tongue, and hardly nobody noticed as the Baron and Panzer took the cylinder down the aisle, turned it on its side, and rolled it under the ring. The only one who did notice, in fact, was a little kid, dressed in a cowboy suit and sitting in his momma's lap.

"So it is in that spirit of unbending competition that I now call to the ring tonight's challenger, weighing three hundred and fifty pounds, from somewhere in Louisiana, THE ANGEL OF SORROW. . . ." Durwood pointed at the main gate, through which stepped Louis Karp. The crowd thought it was funny, but Karp was looking around for guns and knives. Only when he was satisfied that things looked right did he wave the Angel to enter.

"And now the defenders . . . weighing four hundred and seventy pounds of untested fury, Tyler's own HERMAN WARE. . . ." Durwood turned and pointed at the front porch, onto which from the front room stepped a bashful Herman, blushing pink in Seymour's red and white checkered sunsuit. "And last but not least, giving them the combined wrestling weight of six hundred pounds, our very own CLAUDIUS P. GAINS!"

Claudius stepped out and acknowledged the cheers with a sweeping, hat-off, formal bow.

All eyes except Bubba's were on the front porch. Bubba was watching the side of the ring, where from underneath a pair of boy's hands reached out and pulled under two buckets.

Overhead, over where Squint was working, the three wrestlers climbed through the ropes and had the rules read to them—no gouging of the eyes, no biting, kicking, pulling hair, no pulling ears or hitting below the belt, but otherwise, no holds barred and no interruptions after the bell rings. It was to be a fight to the finish, and the finish would be when one side either quit or was rendered incapable of wrestling by the other side.

Durwood Henry, all his announcing done except for the last, which would be when there was a winner, climbed from the ring and stood by the bell. Claudius placed Herman where he and the Angel were facing each other, then nodded to Durwood. Durwood rang the bell, and Herman and the Angel went into semi-squatting defensive positions. Claudius just turned his back on them, waved at the crowd, and crawled through the ropes to a position of safety on the side, and Panzer handed the confident Claudius a bottle of cold beer. He stood there waving at the crowd from time to time, smiling at friends, and drinking beer, while Herman carried out the first part of the plan, tiring the Angel out.

Poor Herman had never wrestled or been in a fight in his whole life; it was probably safe to say that he'd never even been mad at anybody in his whole life, so he was easy prey for the Angel's lightning attacks. The Angel grabbed his right arm by the wrist, held it high, and ducked under it and spun it behind Herman's back in a vicious arm twister, but Herman's body was too big for the Angel to reach around and solidify the hold, and all Herman had to do was turn around. There was the Angel holding his wrist like a little lost boy holding onto his daddy at a big parade. That seemed to make the Angel mad, so the next thing he did was rush in close and grab the shorter Herman in a bear hug. He tried to squeeze the life out of him first, but Herman's insulation was so thick that was impossible. The next thing he tried was lifting Herman off his feet, and that was like wrestling a tree stump out of the ground. He did it; he got Herman up off his feet, but the Angel's legs trembled under the load, and he couldn't do anything with him. Herman, in fact, was tickled by the Angel's face in his stomach.

Step two in the plan was already in progress. Under the ring, Squint had already worked the cylinder to the far corner of the ring and had made two trips back for the buckets. He could tell when the Angel picked up Herman because the ceiling bowed and groaned over him. Squint's main occupation was watching Karp's green cowboy boots, as they moved back and forth around the corner, and waiting for an opportunity.

Upstairs the Angel was working up a sweat. He popped Herman in the chest with a stinging forearm to give him something to think about and hurried over to his corner.

Squint had filled one of the buckets with Slick-ums and was about to make the switch with one of the two water buckets in front of him when the boots suddenly moved around to the bucket side of the corner and Karp's hands came down to saturate a sponge. If Squint had already made the switch and Karp's hand had gone in the bucket of oily-feeling gook, all their plans would have gone right out the window. That's how close they came to disaster.

Suddenly Squint was aware that somebody was under

the ring with him. He had decided to fill the second bucket, had opened the valve at the top of the cylinder, and was holding the hose low in the bucket to keep it from splashing when he looked around to see Bubba staring him in the face. "Shhhhhhhh," Squint whispered, turning off the valve and putting his finger to his lips for secrecy. "Let's play a trick." Bubba was happy to be quiet as there was nothing he liked better than a trick.

Karp's boots were on the side away from the buckets; the groaning of the wrestling was on the far side of the ring behind Squint, so he made the switch. First one bucket, then the other.

"See those boots over there?" He pointed to the corner of the ring where Panzer and the Baron stood waiting. "Crawl over there real quick and knock on the toes." Squint made a motion with his knuckles like he was knocking on a door, and Bubba took off crawling. Squint watched, and the kid did as he was told. Very deliberately he knocked on first one set of toes and then the other. He crawled back to where Squint was and waited for what came next. Squint kept him quiet by telling him, "Watch those buckets, and when they get picked up, we crawl out over there, and I'll get you a hot dog." The second step of the plan was now completed, and there wasn't anything to do but watch the buckets and wait.

Up until that time Herman had been holding his own, without getting mad, without making the first aggressive move. The Angel tried everything he knew, flying two-footed kicks, going for the fat legs, even slipping around in back and riding Herman like a horse, but he couldn't get him down on the mat, and if he ever did, he wasn't sure he could keep him there. All the time Karp kept hollering out things for the Angel to do: "Hit him in the face; go for his throat!" and things like that. The truth of the matter was the Angel was getting too tired, not just tired of trying to do something with Herman, but tired of everything, of living in that stinking trailer, of eating them stinking beans, of going from one stinking town to another, of beating people up and having everybody scared of him and hating him. What's more, he was getting tired of Karp always telling him what to do and promising him things that never came true.

Over where Claudius was standing, there started to be some activity, and the action in the ring stopped for it. It wasn't an official time-out, but it was like a mutually agreed-on rest, and the Angel, Herman, Karp, indeed, everybody in the arena started watching as Claudius took off his coat and hung it on a hanger and handed it to the Baron. A murmur, then a real cheer went up.

Claudius returned the attention by lifting his arms

up over his head and making little drumstick muscles. He acted like he was going to climb in the ring, and the cheering got louder; then he turned and leaned out from the side of the ring like a swimmer about to dive, and Panzer and the Baron stepped close to him and sprayed him all over with the horrible-smelling bug spray. Claudius endured it. He didn't even vary the lines of his smile, and as far as anybody in the crowd knew, he was getting sprayed with something as nice-smelling as Pine-Sol.

Now this, finally, is where all the thinking, scheming, and downright cheating paid off. Claudius climbed in the ring big as life and walked right up to the Angel and threw himself in the Angel's arms, and the Angel, not being able to think, caught him. Of course, what happened was predictable. The Angel did again what he'd done the first time, dragged Claudius over to the corner where Karp was standing, and Karp did again what he'd done, pitched the bucket of water on Claudius and his wrestler. He didn't even notice that the first bucket wasn't water until the second load was on the way.

That was more than enough. A strange look came on the Angel's face, a look of defeat or resignation, like all of his tiredness and meanness had come to a head and he was glad it was over. He tried to stand up by holding onto Claudius's body, but he continued his steady downward course and was soon lying like a beer-soaked beetle on his back. He kicked his arms and legs as best he could and managed to roll over on his hands and knees, but when he did, his arms and legs slid out from under him, and he was helplessly on his face.

If the Baron or Panzer had thrown the buckets out, the crowd would have shouted, "Cheat," and demanded their money back. As it turned out, Karp had thrown the stuff on both the Angel and Claudius, and the crowd was confused. The carpenter's tacks Claudius had hammered through the soles of his shoes bit into the canvas covering the ring, and so he was able to keep his feet under him; they thought the Angel had suffered a seizure or was suffering from a mad fit of some kind. They didn't know what to think when Claudius bent over and twisted his fingers into the Angel's heavy socks, lifted his legs, and started sliding him on his face back and forth toward the metal corner post where Claudius fully intended to put an end to his wrestling career forever.

Poor Karp was probably the most confused person in the whole arena. Not only could he not think of the right thing to do to help, but he did the very worst thing possible. He thought that maybe the Angel could dry himself off and threw in the towel.

"That's it," Durwood Henry started yelling, both

to the people in the arena and to the fans listening at home. "I never would've believed it, but the Angel's manager, Louis Karp, has called it quits. The final match is over." Durwood was just as confused as everybody. "I don't know why the Angel melted like he did, but all of a sudden all the fight just went out of him, and he couldn't stand up." Durwood was talking more to the folks at home than those in the crowd, but the crowd heard it, and the Baron wasted no time in ringing the bell, and Claudius wasted no time in raising his hands in victory. Herman was down on his hands and knees at the edge of the Slick-ums pool, sniffing it and testing it with his fingers.

47: Aftermath, the End of the Story

The mean business in the ring was over, but something else happened that's worth telling about.

About the same time Karp realized that nobody was going to listen to his protests that he was cheated and gave up, slinking through the crowd and back to his trailer, two cars were converging on Tyler. One of the cars was from Waco, and the other one had come all the way from Galveston.

It had been exactly two weeks and one day since

their sister's funeral, and neither Aunt Lucille nor Aunt Viola had slept a whole night through without worrying about Constance's poor children in the hands of the biggest scoundrel the Lord ever put on legs, Claudius Gains. Earlier in the afternoon, in Galveston, Aunt Viola had been listening to *As the World Turns* on the radio, and the story was about a little boy who had amnesia. Suddenly she decided to make a long-distance telephone call to her sister in Waco. "I can't stand it anymore"—she and Aunt Lucille had both been listening to the same show—"I'm going to check on those children." And two and a half hours later Aunt Lucille convinced Uncle George that they too had to go check on those children. What Aunt Lucille actually said was, "Get in the car, George, OR ELSE." George didn't have to ask what "or else" meant to know it would be something bad.

That made the timing perfect because Waco is exactly two and a half hours closer to Tyler than Galveston. When George pulled his car onto the blacktop road leading to the old farm, first he marveled at all the vehicles coming down the road toward him: cars, buses, trucks, tractors, even an ambulance or two. Then he notice the car in front. Aunt Lucille declared, "Ain't that Viola and Claude's car ahead of us?" George declared that he thought it was.

A few buses, cars, and trucks were still leaving the

arena as the two cars carrying the aunts and uncles started up the dirt trail toward it, but the vehicles were no longer important. The aunts and uncles were agape at the sight of the arena by that time. They saw the billboard for Nature's Aid Foundation Garments, and the one of Sheriff Burl Jernigen, and the pair of giant hairy feet. In the first car, Aunt Viola said, "I think I'm gonna faint," but she didn't.

In the second car, Aunt Lucille said, "They ought to lock Claudius Gains up in prison."

They had no earthly idea what was going on, of course, not even enough of an idea to make a bad guess. When the cars stopped at the main gate and the first person they saw was the Mask with that pillowcase over his head like an executioner, and the second person they saw was the Claw with that sock on the end of his arm, the only thing they could think was too terrible to put into words. Both aunts fainted.

They fainted a second time when Seymour came running out to say hello and almost fainted a third time when they actually got inside the arena and saw Claudius, still wearing his wrestling outfit, hosing the Slick-ums off the Angel of Sorrow so the big man could stand up.

And that's all there is to say, except that it took some cooling and golden words to settle the two aunts down that night. Squint did his best, saying how he was happier than he'd ever been before in his life, and Julie did her best, saying how she was in love with the man with the pillowcase over his head, and how he was going to become the Golden Hawk, and how they were going to get married. Claudius showed them the money they'd made by putting on the matches, more money than either Uncle George or Uncle Claude had ever seen in their lives, enough to pay off the bank and then some.

It sounds mean to say, but Aunt Viola and Aunt Lucille had both been hoping to find the kids destitute, or stricken by amnesia or something, and willing to make a choice between the two of them. There wasn't any way to hide the disappointment they felt at finding everything all right.

Claudius offered them a room in the house to spend the night. Uncle George and Uncle Claude both liked wrestling and would've stuck around for a while, but the aunts wanted no part of it. "Say what you think we ought to do, George," Aunt Lucille ordered.

Uncle George pulled on his ear and his nose and said, "Don't seem like anything we can do but head on back home." And that's exactly what they did.

☐ EPILOGUE ☐

For Those Who Want
to Know What Happened

What happened was what you thought might happen. Claudius went down to the bank the next morning and paid off the ghouls, and people started leading normal lives.

Nothing more was heard from the aunts and uncles except fond remembrances at Christmas, Thanksgiving, and Easter.

McKay Brothers eventually lost his amusement park

to the forces of progress, and retired with Seymour to Anaheim, California.

Sheriff Burl Jernigen got reelected and lived out three more terms in office.

Deacon Lawrence Rambo stayed pretty much the same, except that he took to dyeing his hair black and started radio preaching.

The kid, Bubba, grew up and became the first member of his clan to get through college and dentistry school.

What else is there? Except you'll want to know what happened to the Angel of Sorrow. Claudius talked to him and convinced him (with a minimum of effort) that he could enroll in the Gains Internationally Famous Wrestling College of Tyler, Texas, and sleep in his own bed in the basement, and eat Herman's cooking, and even change his name to something like Arthur of Old, a name with favorable connotations. The Angel and Herman eventually became good friends, and Herman taught him how to cook.

Karp drove away in the trailer alone, never even looking back.

Someone came along and invented television. There was a Korean War and a Vietnam War, and in between, a whole lot of other things happened.

Julie and the Hawk got married.

Durwood Henry moved into the big time, got a

regular radio announcer's voice, moved to Atlanta, and forgot his old friends.

The Claw wrestled for a few years as the Golden Claw; then he met a young heifer of a girl who sent him spinning. He quit wrestling eventually to start raising sweet potatoes. He'd walk up and down the rows with his happy wife and children behind him, snipping off sucker bugs with his golden claw.

The Good News Choir and Men's Auxiliary Quartet got to be on the *Ed Sullivan Show,* sang "There Is a Hole in Yonder Mountain," and got a good round of applause.

The Baron, Panzer, Betty, and Rose got old, and they helped Claudius and Squint keep things together through the hard times that lay ahead; then eventually they went the way of Constance. There wasn't nothing to be said about it, except that they got what they wanted, a home to retire to and the pleasure of their declining years. You still see their kids and grandkids wrestling sometimes on television, but it's not the same as being there in person.

There remains only the question: What happened to Claudius and Squint?

Well, Claudius was not your usual man. His prophecy came true, and he was remembered thereafter as the man who had defeated the Angel of Sorrow, and for a while people paid him money to say he drank their beer, wore their socks, and sprayed their sweet-smelling chemicals under his arms. But that didn't last long.

And over the next ten years of keeping things together, he kept hearing wild wolves howling, and one morning in the spring Squint called him down to breakfast and got no answer. All his bags were packed, and Claudius was somewhere gone.

Squint, in the meantime, grew up. He got through high school and most of college, then, when he was all alone, sold everything for what he could get for it and went to Florida, where he wanted to go in the first place.